The President

Also by John Stewart

Three historical novels
The Centurion
Last Romans
Marsilio

Two biographies
Standing for Justice
A Promise Kept

One political novel
Visitors

The President

John Stewart

SHEPHEARD-WALWYN (PUBLISHERS) LTD

First published in 2008 by
Shepheard-Walwyn (Publishers) Ltd
15 Alder Road
London SW14 8ER

British Library Cataloguing in Publication Data
A catalogue record of this book
is available from the British Library

ISBN-13: 978-0-85683-261-1

Typeset by Heavens and Earth Art,
Alderton, Suffolk
Printed and bound through
s|s|media limited, Wallington, Surrey

Dedication

To those
who strive to keep the flame of justice burning

Acknowledgements

As with *Visitors*, I am grateful to David Triggs and Tommas Graves for their enthusiasm and support. I am also grateful to Brian Hodgkinson for his ready encouragement, and to Arthur Farndell, for the far from insubstantial task of proof reading. Also my thanks are due to Paul Palmarozza for checking the text and for his most helpful advice.

To my publisher, Anthony Werner, who witnessed the book emerge chapter by chapter, my thanks and grateful appreciation. And to Emma Aldous for her careful marshalling of the contents.

My thanks also to the Henry George Foundation of Great Britain for their support.

Contents

Prologue

The President was missing. Every corner of the White House had been checked and double-checked, but without success. The Vice-President was in Europe. He had not been called, for everyone expected the President suddenly to appear and of course an unnecessary fuss was the last thing that they wanted. The whole situation was most odd, for the President rarely had a moment to himself. Indeed, it seemed that every second of his day was monitored. Yet, after breakfast, he had simply disappeared.

The White House Chief of Staff was in a quandary but just when he had at last decided to go public, the phone rang. The President had been found sitting on a park bench near the Lincoln Memorial.

Chapter One

The limo drew to a sudden stop and the lean grey-haired figure of the White House Chief of Staff jumped out and hurried to where the President was sitting.

'Mr President, are you OK?' he called out anxiously.

'Never better, Joss. Sit down for a moment.'

Joss Johnson obeyed reluctantly.

'I've been watching the people visiting the Memorial. The young ones skip up and come down slowly, and the old crawl up and step out coming down.'

'Well, there's one oldie descending pretty slowly.'

'Another theory in the garbage can!'

'*Are* you all right, Sir? We've been looking for you all morning! In fact, we're all in orbit at the cottage! What happened?'

'It's OK, Joss, I'm not crazy! It was, shall we say, an unusual morning. I had to escape. I'll explain later, but meantime, duty calls. We'd better go back. Sorry to have raised your blood pressure!'

'But, Sir, nobody saw you leave. How did you get out undetected?'

'Joss, I walked out but no one seemed to see me. As I said, it was an unusual morning, but more later.'

John Duncan sprang lightly to his feet. He looked younger than his forty-nine years, though his hair was turning grey.

'The Joint Chiefs have been waiting for some time,' Johnson prompted.

'They're not waiting, Joss. They're talking!'

'You're OK, Sir!'

Both men laughed. Yet Johnson still had disturbing reservations. The US President had acted strangely and that was something he dared not ignore. He needed to know more. What exactly happened this morning? It was an urgent question not to be delayed.

*

By chance the BBC correspondent Sarah Crawford had witnessed the arrival of Joss Johnson and had seen his agitated conversation with the man on the bench who, to her amazement, turned out to be John Duncan. What was going on? There was something very odd about it all, for the tenant of the White House was always surrounded by a posse of thick-necked bodyguards; to be on his own was something very strange indeed. This was a scoop, to say the least, but she felt constrained. Firstly she was BBC and one of the old school and, secondly, she had dined with Joss Johnson and his wife on two occasions. 'Thus conscience doth make cowards of us all,' she muttered to herself. She had better speak to Joss. It was the decent thing.

*

After receiving Sarah Crawford's phone call, Johnson knew he had to act. Luckily he caught the President between meetings and was able to put his case immediately.

Duncan's response was instant and strangely casual. The expected concern about possible political damage was wholly absent.

'Invite her here to supper, tonight if she can make it, and maybe you and Joan could join us. Joss, this isn't an executive order. It doesn't have to be tonight.'

'We're OK, I think, and I know Sarah has been angling for a one-to-one for some time. So I think we've got a date.'

'Let's hope so, for these media people are usually pretty busy,' the President responded and again there was the same casual unconcerned air. This wasn't the usual Duncan.

Joss, though, was sure that Sarah Crawford wouldn't miss the opportunity. 'I'll tell her about your wine cellar!'

'Now I know the reason that you're the Chief of Staff!'

A gentle knock heralded the President's next appointment and Joss took his leave. As he walked to his office, Johnson was pensive. His boss was still quick and efficient but Joss had the strong impression that he didn't seem to care. It was as if nothing mattered. Yet Joss couldn't fault him, for he had dealt with the Crawford matter without the slightest hesitation. Tonight, perhaps, all would be revealed.

Thank God she did the decent thing, Sarah reflected. For so easily the journalistic instinct for a story could have won. Then, how could she have looked Joss Johnson in the eye, or Duncan for that matter? Now she was having supper with the President and his Chief of Staff. Decency had paid her dividend.

What was she going to wear? She smiled at the rise of the familiar mantra for she knew exactly what dress would be appropriate. Then she laughed when she thought of all the innuendo and the clever sniping at her too-nice image. Her colleagues at the Beeb would have to think again, for dinner with the President was real 'hard copy'.

Sarah Crawford was not the only one who was observing at the Lincoln Memorial. Just before setting out for his White House dinner appointment, Joss received a call from a trusted press insider. A tabloid was running a story in their early edition, headed 'Duncan goes AWOL.' Johnson was livid and phoned the editor but, of course, it made no difference. The story was the thing and the people had the right to be informed.

'Hogwash!' Johnson grated as he slammed the phone down.

Chapter Two

'What elegance and dignity', the President called out graciously as his three guests arrived together. 'But, Joss, I sense a note of trouble.'

'A phone call just before we left – a tabloid's running a story in the morning edition.'

'Yes, the press boys told me. I've gone AWOL, I believe! Well, Joss, if the press play hard ball with Billy at tomorrow's briefing, I'll call by and do a little plain speaking. Sorry, ladies. I'm afraid talking 'shop' is the local hazard here! Well, what would you like to drink? The White House is well stocked with all sorts of goodies. Sarah?'

Johnson almost shook his head. This AWOL business could be very awkward, if not damaging, but his friend the President didn't seem to mind. Something had definitely happened in the morning after breakfast: an event strong enough to affect the thinking process of the President and Commander-in-Chief of the most awesome military force in the world. This was not something to dismiss in a dreamy glow of sentimental loyalty.

Sarah chose sherry, and the rest followed her example. Easy pleasantries flowed, but Duncan knew his guests were too polite to probe him on his 'disappearance'. He would have to bring the matter up, and he would, of course, but not quite yet.

Just when the cook indicated that the first course was due, an aide entered with a portable phone.

'Sorry to interrupt, Mr President: it's Secretary of State Anderson; he says it's urgent.'

'Excuse me, folks. It's the usual pre-dinner crisis. Sometimes I think there's someone up there playing tricks!'

Conversation died as Duncan moved out of earshot.

'That's the Presidency!' Joss said knowingly. 'It's 24/7 and it's relentless.'

'I wonder what part of the world it is this time?' his wife questioned.

'Joan, possibilities abound,' her husband responded.

Sarah was fascinated. This was it, the high table, as it were, and her journalistic instincts were on fire.

'That was Andy Anderson,' the President said as he returned. 'Some holy shrine has been stormed by an Islamist cult and the ruling potentate has imposed a news black out. In the absence of information we're being blamed and our Embassy's under attack. Sometimes I think we're the world's fall guy!'

'Is the Embassy staff in danger?' Sarah asked.

'Luckily there's a strong contingent of marines and tear-gas by the gallon. The rioters don't play the Geneva tune but our fellas have body armour and they don't take too many chances. Hopefully it'll blow over soon. But no doubt we'll be blamed for over-reaction. It's the current mind-set.'

'We have our mind-sets too, Sir. I know in Britain we have the 'chattering class' on one side and the 'hard liners' on the other and they're both as blinkered as they come!'

'Sarah, it's a universal failing both individually and collectively. Too often we're as blind as bats. Now to important matters: here comes the first course! We'd better take our seats.'

'This is delicious!' Sarah reacted after her first mouthful.

'Jilly, my housekeeper, is a very good cook. If you could say a quiet word afterwards, it would be good. Such things make the world go round.'

All this was brilliant stuff for a profile, Sarah mused. Then she cringed. How mercenary! Profiting from the occasion seemed so self-serving. Still, it was her profession.

'May I pursue this question of mind-sets?'

'Of course!'

'Well, Sir, if we are all imprisoned in our various mind-sets, it would seem we are all to some extent "seeing through a glass darkly" and certainly "not face to face." So, in fact we are not seeing things as they truly are.'

'I would agree with you, Sarah, but I fear the academics would shred us!'

'How so, Sir?'

'Well, to them "things as they truly are" would be a relative concept.'

'I see their point, but I feel happier with *Corinthians!* That, of course, would be my mind-set.'

They all laughed.

'This certainly is a new line in dinner conversation!' Joss quipped.

'There is one proof that the academics tend to dismiss,' the President continued.

'What is that, Sir?' Sarah pressed.

'Experience.'

'But surely that is the most relative thing there is!'

'Generally that is true, but I feel that most do experience a moment or moments of clarity and the strange thing is, we recognise that clarity.'

'I know what you're saying, Sir, but it's still a relative world,' Joss interjected.

'It is, if you're wedded to empirical proof. However, my proposition is that experience of clarity can be confirmed. Many have recorded their experiences and they all accord. They all say the same. Here I rest my case, for I see with blinding clarity that the second course is coming!'

'To that I raise no objection!'

Again they laughed.

'This is most enjoyable,' the President said easily. 'Sarah, Joss tells me that you would like a one-to-one.'

'Yes, Mr President, that would be wonderful. In fact, landing such an interview might persuade the Beeb to keep me on their books!'

'Surely you've no trouble in that quarter!'

'I'm old-fashioned, they say, and I'm not aggressive enough. That's the usual mantra.'

'There you are, a typical mind-set. Well, this looks good. Jilly's done us proud.'

'And how!' Joan Johnson echoed.

'Hey, it's time to freshen up your glasses. Let me get another bottle,' he added, making to get up.

'Allow me, Mr President.' Joss cut in.

'Sit down, Joss. I'm the host tonight!'

Both men burst out laughing.

'I'm told you both were old school pals,' Sarah ventured.

'Indeed we were, and Joss still bosses me around!' Duncan returned.

'I'd be lucky!' Joss flashed back.

There was more laughter and Sarah suddenly realized that she'd forgotten about the Lincoln Memorial business. Anyway, she didn't feel it was her place to bring it up. Instead, she asked about the forthcoming election.

'We're ahead of the Republican front-runner, Whiteside, at the moment,' the President began, 'but you never can be sure until you cross the line!'

'This front-runner, how popular is he?'

'Whiteside's a fair-haired all-American sort of fella with a pretty wife and one of each, in fact, the perfect candidate. I've met him once or twice. He has a pleasant easy nature.'

'Yeah,' Joss spat, 'but his campaign manager's a first-class bastard.'

'Campaign managers are rarely angels, Joss: except you, of course!'

'I'm glad you noticed, Sir!'

Duncan chuckled.

'Well, I've got news for you!' Joan Johnson quipped.

'Sarah,' the President began, 'I lost my wife three years ago and these good people practically carried me. Indeed, they spend more time here than their own home. So we're close and you, by your integrity this afternoon, are welcome to this band of trust.'

'I am honoured, Sir.'

'And so are we! Now, what happened this morning and why did I suddenly disappear? The simple answer is I felt it necessary to escape this gilded prison that is 1600 Pennsylvania Avenue. But that's not the whole story, of course. This morning I had a touch of what Churchill called his 'black dog'. Now, I wouldn't claim to compete with the great man, but let's say it was pretty dark. All seemed so pointless, repetitive and mechanical. Then I thought of my late wife, which, as you can imagine, didn't help. For some time I sat locked in this arid world until I suddenly realized that the misery was being watched and that this watcher fella was on the side lines unaffected, just like a spectator at a ball game. It was like throwing a switch. Suddenly the world lit up. Everything seemed significant: chairs, table, and cups, even a piece of torn paper lying on the floor. I looked outside; it was a wonderland. So I went downstairs and out into the rose garden. For some strange reason, the usual 'Good morning, Mr President,' was absent. It was as if I'd slipped the net! Outside the wonder hadn't lessened. There was a gardener busy at his work. Normally I would have simply seen a gardener, but this time I saw care and dedication.

'Then I had a naughty-boy desire to roam outside the grounds.

Also I wanted to see the people without them staring at the usual bodyguard screen. It worked; the gods were on my side and there I was, free and fascinated by everything about me. I had had enough sense to grab a baseball cap before I left the Cottage and this I pulled well over my eyes. So I was camouflaged, as it were. Are you all asleep?' Duncan suddenly asked.

'I'm on the edge of my seat, Mr President,' Sarah returned. 'Please go on. What about the people that you met?'

'I felt very much at one with them. We shared a common humanity. It was as if we knew the same secret. Only the mind-sets were different. These were obvious but they were accepted. There was no criticism, though it was hovering. In fact, the light was lessening; even so, I still felt a sense of freedom. We get so worked up about things, and it's so unnecessary. But there are dark souls. I saw one. Such men can be dangerous. There you are, I'm still the same John Duncan but with my mind-set slightly modified. I'm sorry about the trouble that I caused, but I feel the President of the United States needed the experience.'

'Well you've put *my* mind at rest,' Joss responded. 'It's the Press Corps in the morning that concerns me. What should we tell them?'

'Joss, what I did was something many leaders have done throughout the ages. I escaped the magic circle and saw the people face to face. I know it could be viewed as irresponsible. But I feel the American people would prefer their president to be modestly adventurous!'

'That may be optimistic!'

'Let's not apologize too much. I wanted to escape the gilded cage, so I went for a walk! Ah, I see more trouble. '

They all could see the aide approaching with the portable. This time Duncan didn't leave the table.

'Ah, Jim. Good to hear from you... That's a generous offer. I'll pass it on to Andy right away. Hey, when are you coming over? I always value our pow-wows... Yeah, next month would be fine. Guess who is in my dining party this evening... All right, I'll tell you. Sarah Crawford, a fellow Brit... I agree, the best of the best! Hey, the dessert is coming. Make yourself scarce, fella!' The crackle of laughter was audible. 'Next month, then... Good night, Prime Minister – hey, have you lost the art of sleeping. With you it's the middle of the night... sleeping on a plane has never been an art I've mastered. Bye.'

'Well, that was Sir James Babbington, your PM: he thinks I should run the risk of a one-to-one with a certain lady!'

Sarah beamed.

Chapter Three

All at once, it seemed, the President's guests were gone, and the jollity of the evening, suddenly absent, made the silence almost physical. This was the difficult time when the absence of his wife bit deep. Tonight, though, it was different. He even felt a sense of guilt, but the truth was simple. Fair-haired and graceful, Sarah Crawford was delightful, and what a voice, so rich, and yet so unpretentious. Crawford was her maiden name. She had been married but it was said of her husband that he grew much more attached to alcohol than to her. There lay a tragedy. As his friend the Brit PM had said, 'She was the best of the best.' Joan wouldn't mind, he thought, thinking of his past wife. She would understand, but the tug of loyalty was strong.

It had been a remarkable day. He had been foolish wandering off like that, yet, if the truth were known, he wouldn't change a dot or comma. And that strange sense of watching: and it was still there watching, like a presence. Of course, 'that man's got real presence'. It was common parlance. Some people even told him that he had it: but taking that too seriously was the freeway to pomposity.

It was much too soon to go to bed, so he pressed the remote, hoping for the latest news, or spin, which was more like it. Well, if he were a journalist he would be doing just the same. All that airtime to cover, for the viewing public would not tolerate an empty screen. The same went for newspapers, though they'd gone over the top with supplements.

'There it is,' he muttered. He'd given the White House staff a shock, the newsreader reported. He'd simply disappeared and later turned up on a park bench in the Mall. Reliable sources have hinted that the Secret Service wasn't far away. 'Pure invention,' Duncan mouthed. A good line, though, but the idea of hiding behind a lie was abhorrent. Anyway, if he used such an excuse the White House would know of his deception and that simply wasn't on.

He pressed the remote and the screen went black. Then stretching to the side table he scanned the schedule for the following day. There were the usual meetings with Joss and the Press Secretary, Billy Benson. The AWOL President could make that lively! It was tedious, but he'd probably have to intervene at the press briefing. One thing was certain: there would be no grovelling apologies. Fear of terrorism was closing our open society. Vigilance was the duty and the need, not debilitating fear. What else? Oh yes, a report from the Satellite Defence Shield Committee. That was the trouble with technology: the more sophisticated it became, the more advanced became the methods of destruction.

As usual, it was a busy day. But it was the report of the energy think tank that was his priority. A new fuel for the future was the crying need but nature was hiding her secrets well. He sat back in his easy chair. The whole frantic scramble that seemed to typify the nation's life appeared pointless. It was as though everyone was running down the same corridor, forgetting there was ample space on either side. Few thought to stand and stare. This morning's venture in the Mall had made this obvious. He had felt tantalizingly close to something when he sat before the Memorial and now that feeling had returned. Nature had laws, and man desires and needs. The harmony of the two was practical and the obvious course of reason. Science by necessity had discovered such harmonies, but our social skills lagged well behind, for, by the inequity and poverty that abounded, this was clear to see. Somehow we were pushing the rolling stone uphill!

He yawned; suddenly it felt as if his fuel tanks had drained. Duncan, time for bed.

*

Sarah Crawford couldn't sleep. Dinner at the White House had been much too stimulating. The President was fascinating and not a man to pigeonhole. Physically he was handsome, with well-chiselled features and also he was moderately tall. He had to be tough, for the Presidential race was not for wimps, yet he didn't give the sense of being coarsened by the battle. He was his own man. That was obvious enough, but he was not inflexible. She liked him, indeed, she felt attracted, though she didn't stoke the fire. She was mature enough to know how foolish that could be. Anyway, the one-to-one was in the bag and that was quite a coup.

Much too wide-awake, she wondered how he'd handle

questions on his disappearance at the morning press conference. Almost certainly he would have to appear. Seemingly, he didn't seem concerned. She was entitled to attend the press briefings, but decided that a discreet absence was her better part. Someone might have heard of her White House invitation and related questions surfacing at the briefing could be most embarrassing. At least that was how she felt.

Although she was elated by the promise of a one-to-one, her media life no longer satisfied. In many ways she-had-been-there-and-done-it-all and that perhaps was what the Beeb had sensed. She didn't hate her job, far from it, for she met most interesting people. Yet more and more she felt the need for change. Maybe she would write. Her name would help to sell a book or two, at least get the process going. But all her publisher friends had cautionary words. The book world wasn't easy.

At last she felt a drowsiness descend. Yes, it had been a wonderful evening.

Joss Johnson and his wife had noted the obvious rapport between their friend the President and Sarah Crawford. Sarah, of course, was English. She was most attractive. However, any liaison in an election year was fraught with danger and being English, what's-wrong-with-our-American-gals could grow to be a factor. The whole thing made Joss uneasy. Of course, in normal circumstances, such a match would be a blessing, but the Presidential election wasn't normal. Again, with Sarah in the frame, there would be two lives now to trawl for hidden skeletons. John Duncan was a good man, and a second term should not be sacrificed.

Chapter Four

As Sarah had rightly guessed, the Press Corps sensed a story, and Billy Benson found the arrow questions raining like a medieval siege. The President, who had been listening out of vision, knew he had to intervene.

'Good morning, Mr President,' was the chorus greeting.

'You've been giving Billy here a lot of stick. Let's have it straight!'

'What happened yesterday, Mr President? Why did you disappear?'

'Joe, I wish I knew the trick!'

'You disappoint me ,Sir, for I did expect a puff of smoke!'

Duncan laughed. Joe Burns from the *Washington Post* was quick and always likeable.

'Sometimes, Joe, I wouldn't mind a smokescreen. But hey, I haven't given you an answer and you deserve one; in fact, you all do. It's simple, and I make no apologies at all. I went for a walk and, contrary to the news report, the Secret Service wasn't in attendance.'

There was a sudden storm of interjections and Sarah Crawford, who was watching at home, realized that John Duncan was going to tell it as it was: a high-risk policy with that mob doing their best to savage you.

'OK, guys, I hear you and I can tell you that I didn't rob a bank or take the GOP frontrunner hostage. I just went for a walk, OK! Yesterday morning I woke up feeling down in the dumps. Then I saw this down-in-the-dumps fella was doing a little wallowing. I guess we all recognize the picture. Well, I gave this tedious guy the slip and the world lit up. It was a lovely morning, as you may remember, and resplendent with the colours of the fall, so I wandered out into the rose garden. Henry the gardener was busy but he didn't see me and I didn't interrupt. Normally I chirp a greeting, but this time I saw his care and dedication and it alerted me sufficiently to remember the words of Emerson, about the human family being bathed in an element of love. I recommend his essay on friendship.'

Sarah was amazed, for the press corps was completely silent.

'I didn't decide to go outside. I simply found myself outside and I hired a taxi. I must say I pulled the baseball cap I had, well down. I was only in the taxi a minute before I realized I had no money, cards or any means of payment. So I stopped the driver and apologized.

'"It's OK, man, I've done the same myself. Where do you wanna go? It's on me." So there you are, another touch of Emerson. I took his number, so he'll get a surprise present.'

'This mode continued. One elderly man recognized me, I think, but he just said, "Good morning, Sir," and discreetly went his way. Then Joss Johnson arrived. At first I couldn't understand why he was so agitated, but I quickly got the message. Ladies and gentlemen of the press, this was the first time in three years that I had truly met the people, without the usual Presidential trappings. It was stimulating and very heartening. I only saw one dark soul nursing his resentment. All the rest responded openly. It was an inspiring morning and one I wouldn't be without. Again I make no apology. We are an open society, and the threat of terrorism induces fear. Vigilance is vital, as are sensible precautions, but fear weakens and debilitates. Thank you, folks, that's it this morning!'

A stunned silence held until the President left and then the buzz of conversation rose in volume. Billy Benson took his place and the briefing session continued.

Sarah was thoughtful as she sat back in her easy chair. He had won the battle but the skirmishes would continue. The opposition element was bound to milk it. Indeed, her journalistic instincts told her it was borderline, with cynics competing with their withering headlines. Yet there was something almost noble in the honesty of his answer and the reference to Emerson was bound to have a positive effect. Americans might even dust their volumes of the great New Englander and read them.

All was going well for Senator Sam Whitehead, the Republican front-runner. Indeed, his position, according to the polls, was unassailable and the confidence of his campaign manager, Ed Vince, reflected this. The two men were very different. Whitehead was cool and deliberate, not a fool by any means, yet sometimes slow to seize his opportunities. Vince was the opposite. Hard-headed and impulsive, he rarely failed to spot an opening that could weaken an opponent. In fact, he was a master of negative campaigning. Too many policy statements meant too many commitments and they were best avoided.

'Senator, it's time we attacked Duncan. I've been saying it for weeks but you've been playing Mr Nice Guy. But now we have an opportunity. Dammit, we can't miss it, Sam. The guy's the President of Fairyland.'

'Ed, I saw the press briefing and I agreed with Duncan. I thought he was impressive.'

'Jeez, Senator, that's not the point. Duncan's laid himself open. He deserves a salvo!'

'Maybe, but it's a dirty business.'

'So you won't attack?'

'Not on this issue.'

'Well, there's always the press.'

Whitehead said nothing, but he wasn't pleased.

'President of Fairyland' was the headline in a Chicago morning edition. 'Dreamy Duncan Deserts Post' was another, this time from the South. The supporting reports were both vindictive in their passion. 'The Walkabout President,' was the milder headline from a New York paper. Few were positive, but those who were, plainly understood the President's message. Joe Burns, for one, wrote a clearly supportive article.

Joss hoped the whole thing would simply fade away, but that he knew was wishful thinking. The President, though, was still bullish. To him the passion of the opposition was a proof his words had found their target.

Johnson had almost finished scanning the papers when he saw the headline on the inside pages. 'Ace BBC correspondent, Sarah Crawford, dines with the President.'

'Jeez,' Joss exhaled. 'How do they do it?'

Chapter Five

Although the AWOL incident soon receded from front page of the newspapers, it was still prominent in the President's mind. The lit-up state that he'd briefly experienced had disturbed complacency. He wanted to know more and, of course, he wanted the experience to repeat, but he knew enough to know such things were not commanded. The desire to share his private thoughts and questions was strong but somehow there was no one he could turn to. Since he'd lost his wife he had no close family and his life-long friend, Joss Johnson, was much too focused on the politics of the day. The Presidency was a solitary role, and unguarded asides were a luxury he didn't have. Casual remarks too easily ended up in people's published diaries.

The Presidency demanded wakefulness, and a supreme wakefulness was what he had experienced on his 'disappearance'. Here, if they arose, unguarded comments didn't find expression. The lit-up state made sure of that.

Some of the brightest minds worked in the White House. Many of them, he felt sure, would have understood his questions. But he felt constrained. He was the chief, the President. It was his role, the part that he was duty-bound to play.

It was Harry, the driver of the limo, who first broke the spell of his isolation. Harry was an ex-Marine Sergeant, a big man and usually brief in conversation. Normally there was little opportunity to talk, especially with the Secret Service man present, but on this occasion they were standing by the car together prior to setting off.

'I liked what you said at the Press briefing the other day, Mr President.'

'Thank you, Harry.'

'I had a similar experience once myself.'

'Your army days?'

'Yes, Sir. I had almost finished my tour when it happened and when I got home, I went straight to the library and tried to find out what had really happened.'

'Did you?'

'No, but the librarian put me on to someone who was attending a discussion group.'

'And you went along?'

'Yes, Sir, and I've been turning up ever since.'

'Clearly you have found it helpful. What have you discovered?'

'That I'm mostly asleep, Sir, but we have an exercise where we sit and let the mental buzz subside. In fact, we get real still at times.'

'Ah, here are the Secret Service boys – we're off again. Harry, thanks for that. Maybe we can have a sandwich together some lunchtime.'

'That would be great, Sir,' Harry replied, somewhat overwhelmed.

The President was thoughtful as the limo glided off. He sat back in his seat. Harry had clearly recognized what he, John Duncan, had experienced, despite the fact he'd toned it down to suit the briefing. Strange though, Harry had been the only one to make it plain he understood. He'd had many complimentary words, but that was for political savvy. The whirlpool of the White House day left little room for reflection, and Duncan knew that he was caught up in the swirl like all the rest. Strange indeed that no one had responded to his mention of Emerson and the fine oil of humanity he called love. Maybe they thought that it was play-school stuff: an embarrassing touch of sentimentality. Well, they hadn't heard the end of it. The Walk in the Mall, as he thought of it, had alerted him. One theme kept returning, even though he didn't really understand it. That was the need for harmony between the natural law and human society. Very grand, Duncan, his cynical side reacted. Yet something strong and certain would not let the matter rest.

Sarah had had no contact with the White House since the dinner party, but she knew the one-to-one would happen in good time. Meantime she studied all John Duncan's statements. Most were particular in their nature but occasionally there were the broader statements of policy. Tonight he was the guest at a dinner for corporate heads at a Washington hotel; the cost per plate was earmarked for a charitable foundation. She had received a press pass, so she would be there in person. The audience were to a man, and woman, well-heeled corporation heads: a hard-bitten lot, in her estimation, with share price as their bottom line. She wondered what John Duncan's line would be. Would he butter them up, as expected in an election year, or would he plough a different furrow? She would soon know.

Only God knew what the cost per plate would be. Corporate bosses had deep pockets. The guests gathered slowly, taking their positions at the array of tastefully decorated round tables. Sarah was sitting with fellow media folk including Joe Burns, who was for once subdued. Sarah guessed he didn't like such gatherings. 'The dollar obesity club,' he had muttered.

Suddenly there he was, weaving between the tables, a wave here, a handshake there. It was good old political fare, but the apparent bonhomie of the President's arrival belied John Duncan's state of mind. Troubled by a strong aversion to the whole event, Duncan viewed the speech he had prepared as insincere and sycophantic. Even in the limo he had struggled with the text, testing the patience of his long-suffering speechwriter who had travelled with him.

As is customary, the Chairman opened with a few brief welcoming words, after which grace was said. Then an army of waiters and waitresses descended and the meal began. The build-up of aversion continued. He couldn't seem to shake it off. Was he going 'bloody bonkers', as his friend the Brit PM was wont to say, and was his mood related to what had happened the other morning?

Did it really matter what he said? These corporate guys had hides like body armour. Little would get through. The problem was the TV coverage, for whatever he said was flashed around the world by CNN. There was no hiding place for the US President and media scrutiny was like a permanent X-ray.

Duncan's host had been indicating some of the principal guests and, distracted as he was, the President's attention had been partial. His host, an elderly grey-haired banker, had now turned to the broader subject of the economy. He was concerned with the growing maze of corporate regulations. Tax was a nightmare and the need for simplicity was crying out. The President nodded in agreement, but he still was distracted and could not seem to focus.

'Someone needs to speak out,' the banker said forcefully. 'We need a new direction and someone needs to speak the truth!'

The words hit Duncan almost physically.

The dinner was over and an aide was placing a lectern on the table before him.

A copy of his speech was left before him. An aide was placing the auto cue. Suddenly Duncan told him to remove it. The uncertainty had gone and in its place was an unerring confidence. It was not the pumped-up stuff Duncan noticed, but a simple surety.

With the preliminaries now over, the President rose. There was so much space.

Duncan began thanking everyone for their support and praising the corporate enterprise which they represented. It was what everyone expected; predictable plaudits to keep everyone content. Sarah groaned inwardly as the litany continued. The universal thank-you speech. God, she'd heard so many. Joe Burns seemed to have shrunk; no doubt, he was suffering too! After what seemed an age, the tone suddenly changed.

'We are living in an age of touch screen technology and global trading. Such trading seeks the cheapest unit of production where subsistence wages give the chosen factory edge. Indeed, a philanthropic company intent on hiking social standards could lose their market all too easily. Such are the problems of this global age and it's to you I turn for help. Can we bring humanity to the global workplace? Again, can we bring humanity to our own domestic scene? Why does grinding poverty still cohabit with abundant riches?

'The President of the United States is the President of both the rich and poor and because of this it is incumbent that I look for answers.'

The President had the full attention of the hall. Sarah was all too aware that his words could well be seen as grossly insensitive, if not dangerous politically. Criticizing lions in their den was hardly politic. Yet, as far as she could see, there was no resentment.

'The Roman, Cicero, said, and here I paraphrase, that every man's wealth should correspond to his service to the community. In fact, the Roman senators were generous in their patronage. Patronage is laudable and it is essential in the arts, but I would suggest we need to look more fundamentally. For instance, there are laws governing the physical world such as gravity. These are quite precise. The question is: What of the laws governing human activity and in particular social and economic behaviour? Of course, some may say there aren't any, or, if there are, they're largely relative. My own belief, or rather instinct, is that there is a harmony between society and nature, just as there is a harmony in relation to the environmental issue. In my opinion, it is this harmony that we need to discover. Doubtless some will say with force – that is your job, Mr President. Well, yes, it is my job, but I believe it's yours as well. Pessimism, and the attitude that the better rule will never work, are both defeatist. But with a steadfast will the ideal, which is a home to reason, can become the practical.'

The President laughed. Sarah was fascinated. He seemed so utterly relaxed and it was crystal clear; he meant exactly what he said. Not something, Sarah guessed, that gatherings such as this experienced often. Too many speeches danced cleverly on the surface without connection with the heart.

'Now I suspect the press will have a little fun tomorrow. But there it is, we aim to please!'

There was an obliging ripple of laughter and once more the President scanned the hall looking into every corner.

'This is a short speech and I'm sorry if you feel you haven't had your money's worth. However, you can blame your worthy chairman for this brevity, for it was he who prompted me to leave my written speech aside. "We need a new direction", he said "and someone needs to speak the truth." I can only hope I did.'

Chapter Six

The President had spotted Sarah as he left accompanied by the usual posse of aides. He waved, but that was hardly private in such a crowded room. Of course, any overt greeting would have been unwise; for one small hint was quite enough to blast gossip-addicted Washington into orbit.

Duncan didn't think much of his speech. It was too short and much too vague. But at least he had avoided the well-worn path of platitude. There was something else. He had been without the slightest qualm and had spoken from himself. There had been no manufactured phrases meant to please one faction or another. That was the strange thing about the evening. The safety-first banalities were forbidden. At least, that was how it seemed. And the persistent aversion: where had that been seeded?

The powerful Wall Street icon and leader of the massive Two Oceans Trading conglomerate, or simply TOT, was far from happy. This President was a dreamer, who had the dangerous knack of asking awkward questions. OK, so there was exploitation! Yeah, big deal, but better that than the goddam desert where the workforce scraped their living. This Duncan guy was out-to-lunch. He could upset the money guys and that was high-risk poker.

The icon turned awkwardly to his neighbour.

'Jake, this fella's a boy scout; we gotta stop him.'

'Yeah, JP, he's up there with the fairies.'

'Those papers that you own: why don't you drop a dump truck of dirt.'

'The guy's too clean. He's goddam lilywhite!'

'Goddammit, invent something! That son-of-bitch is dangerous!'

'Yeah, it could boost the circulation!' Jake laughed thinly; he had no intention of courting libel writs.

'Well, Jake, this show's over. Let's have a shooter at the club.'

'Yeah, you've got it!'

*

'Mr President, do you want a second term?' Joss Johnson reacted when his chief returned to the White House.

'Joss, you should be at home. It's past your bedtime!'

'Mr President, four state governors have been on the phone wondering what's going on! You've introduced a note of uncertainty and it makes people uneasy!'

'Joss, I wasn't advocating a revolution. I was merely suggesting that a more equitable society was desirable. I said very little, Joss. In fact, my speech was far too short.'

'You touched a nerve and a sensitive one at that. God knows what the press will say tomorrow! If you'd used your prepared speech none of this would have happened!'

Duncan could see that his old friend Joss Johnson was upset and had clearly had a difficult evening. He needed to clear the air.

'Joss, without your skill in political management I would not be President. That I acknowledge unreservedly. But, as you would readily agree, there is more to the Presidency than that. My sojourn in the Mall was a kind of wake-up call and since then I've begun to question things. How can we be indifferent to the grinding poverty we see in a land of such abundant wealth? And if we are indifferent, why are we so blind?'

'You were always the visionary.'

'Yes, Joss, perhaps I was. But you were the organizing hand that placed me here in the Oval Office. As they say, it was, and is, a double act!'

'Even a stand-up comedy!' Joss quipped.

'Joss, I believed what I said this evening. The old Chairman was right. We need a new direction! The rich are getting richer and the poor are getting poorer. We can't go on ignoring what's before our eyes!'

'By the way, I got a call from Harry, your driver.'

'It's his night off. When did he call?'

'Just before you arrived – I asked him what it was but he said he'd try again.'

'I bet he listened to the speech. Did he leave his number?'

Joss shook his head.

'Pity, I'd like to phone him back.'

'Allow me, Mr President,' Joss returned, looking wryly at his friend. He lifted the phone.

'Janie, could you get Harry Roberts on the line? He phoned a few minutes ago.' Joss smiled. 'That's how it's done, Mr President. No wonder I'm the Chief of Staff!'

They both laughed, and when the amusement settled, the phone rang.

The President pressed the audio.

'Mr Roberts on the line, Mr Johnson.'

'Harry, it's the President. You were looking for me.'

'Yes, Mr President, I listened to your speech. You meant what you said, Sir!'

'I did, Harry, but how to put it into practice is the question.'

'I have a book that talks about poverty in the midst of progress. If you like I'll bring it in tomorrow, Sir.'

'Thanks Harry, yeah, I'd like to see it. Sounds familiar; a fella bent my ear one evening on the subject. I remember he went on a bit. His hero was an economist called George, but the experts say he's history.'

'True principles are never history, Sir!'

'My God, Harry, you're getting poetical. It must be that Welsh ancestry of yours! Hey, we haven't had that sandwich yet. Let's make it tomorrow. My diary says I have a space at noon.'

'Thank you, Mr President.'

'See you, Harry.'

'Harry's quite a guy. He attends a discussion circle. It seems to be a kind of self-help group, but feet-on-the-ground in nature.'

'And he's an ex-Marine sergeant, I believe.' Joss added.

'Yeah, not a flower-power softie!'

Chapter Seven

Ex-Marine Sergeant Harry Roberts had never been inside the Oval Office before and even though he got on well with the President, he felt nervous. He knew it was just petty fears; they had debated similar situations at the discussion group, but even so it wasn't easy. The choice of living in the midst of swirling thought or in the present was as constant as parade drill used to be. He'd been in harm's way many times. This brought crystal sharpness of attention by necessity, yet here, walking through to the Oval Office, his heart was pumping hard.

'Right on time, Harry: first-timers often fall over the furniture, but you've been through too much for that!'

'My heart is thumping like a rock band, Sir!'

'The weaknesses that flesh is heir to, Harry: my knees still knock before a major speech!'

Harry knew the President was trying to put him at his ease and to a large extent he had succeeded.

'The sandwiches will be coming shortly, but in the meantime where's this book you recommended?'

Harry handed over a package neatly wrapped and the President undid the tape.

'*Progress and Poverty* – the perfect title for this crazy age! Hey, this is a new book!'

'It's a gift, Sir.'

'That's damned nice of you, Harry, but you haven't written anything on the inside page! '

'What should I write?'

'Something simple – to President Duncan with best wishes.'

The President grinned and Harry burst out laughing. All the nerves had gone.

'Now, Harry, you're not just here for the sandwiches. I want a summary, straight from the horse's mouth, as it were. What is the author's message? We've got about twenty minutes.'

'I can dry up much quicker than that, Sir!' He paused, focusing his attention. Here was a golden opportunity to spell out Henry George's message and to the US President himself. He daren't miss the putt, thinking of his golfing hobby.

'Take the old Wild-West town of the movies. In the high street there are the bank, the saloon and the general store. These are the most valuable sites. Now the town grows and, as it does, up goes the value of these very sites. Of course, this value is due, not to the individual owners of the hardware store etc, but to the collective presence of the town itself: in other words, the community. Then think what happens when the high street becomes the centre of a city. The increase in value reaches for the sky. In our present system this value belongs to the fortunate guy who owns the site, but, the truth is, he didn't create it: the presence of the community did. George's principle is to leave sacred to the individual what the individual has created, but render to the community what the community has created. Indeed, this collective value is the natural revenue of the state.'

'Harry, around the Wild-West town there is plenty of space. Everybody can claim a patch. So, how does poverty arise?'

'Those at the centre with high-value property and therefore credit buy up vacant land about the town. Then they simply wait, knowing there'll be further settlers and that these new folk will have to pay them rent, or settle some way distant. Here you have the beginning of the haves and have-nots: those who own their sites and those who rent them. As population swells the situation becomes dire. All the land has been enclosed as private property and the growing numbers now pay more and more for less and less. Meanwhile the high street swells in value. Skyscrapers are born. The collective community value is enormous, but this does not end up in the public purse; instead it is the windfall due to landlords, who by good fortune own the sites. We call it real estate!'

'My God, Harry, that's strong stuff. And you've been driving me around with it under your hat for almost two years! You should have spoken up!'

'Mr President, it wouldn't have been appropriate. Anyway, most switch off when I speak about such things. Your speech last night gave me the lead and the courage to phone.'

'Am I that frightening?'

They both laughed.

'Harry, you heard me fumbling in the dark last evening. If you were President, where would you start?'

'We need to ease the burden of taxation on production and replace the shortfall with a small percentage of location value.'

'By location value you mean?'

'Every site has a value independent of the building on it. That value is due to its location. Take Manhattan, the location value must be astronomic. No individual or corporation could have created that.'

'Jeez, this is dynamite! Have you ever tried to ...?'

'I know what you're going to ask, Sir – nobody wants to know!'

'I know, they all want to be billionaires! Well, Harry, you've infected the President with the virus, so who knows? But it won't be easy, by God it won't.'

There was a knock on the door.

'Where does the time go? Harry, ask Mary to give you an hour slot, tomorrow, if she can. In the meantime, I will start this book.'

They shook hands and Harry Roberts felt his feet were inches off the ground.

The press were divided. 'President takes the moral high ground' and 'President calls for a new direction,' were positive but colourless, while the critical headlines were, as often is the case, much more entertaining: 'AWOL President – second act,' and 'Not another new frontier!' However, a guest article in the *New York Times* by BBC correspondent Sarah Crawford drew a different picture. The President was not content with empty words. He wanted action and a new direction, which would seek a harmony between society and nature. Was this his election message?

Chapter Eight

Ed Vince burst noisily into Senator Whitehead's office. Energy spilled from him like beer carried by a careless hand.

'JP Sebbson, or Seb to us, has landed the big one. He's spread the rumour that Duncan's sweet on the Crawford dame. Duncan has dined with her and she gushed with praise for Duncan on last night's prime time chat show. Seb's leaned on some editor fella. So tomorrow morning should be interesting.'

'Ed, I don't want anything to do with Sebbson or his games. He's a first-class bastard.'

'Yeah, but a mega donor – Seb's been real useful.'

'Maybe, but favours from that guy makes me nervous. For him it's not strings attached, it's goddam cables! Keep him in the back seat, Ed, and don't accept any more of his cash.'

'He could get vindictive, for he's got an ego bigger than the Empire State!'

'Yeah, tell me something I don't know! Listen, Ed, we play clean. That's the bottom line – period.'

Ed Vince was frustrated, yet he was attracted to his Chief's honesty. Indeed Ed was not unlike a moth attracted to the flame. The trouble was the light of honesty and the quicksilver of clever dishonesty were both a draw. Ed-should-go had never quite translated to Ed-must-go, for just when Sam Whitehead had resolved to act, Ed would prove his worth with some remarkable burst of industry. And of course, he was a likeable devil.

Sarah Crawford sat transfixed. It wasn't happening, it couldn't be real, but there it was, in bold type on the front page and with her photograph. The headline was devastatingly simple: 'The President has a Girlfriend!' She should have been outraged, but she wasn't, for the truth was, she rather liked John Duncan. Then with unrelenting force her predicament closed over her. She was a journalist; she knew the game and all its tricks too well. Already, they would be waiting at the door. She went to the window of her first-floor apartment and stood to the side and behind the fine mesh curtain. Yes, there they were!

*

'Joss, this is pure invention', the President burst out, tossing the tabloid in his Chief of Staff's direction.

'Yeah, but it's damned good fiction! In fact, it's close to faction!'

'What are you saying, Joss?'

'I'm saying that you're both fond. It was obvious at the dinner party. Ed Vince, or whoever is behind this "revelation", has pushed the boat out from the moorings. You can't just drift, you gotta set a course!'

'Jeez, Joss, this isn't Vegas!'

'No, Sir, it's worse!'

Duncan shook his head.

'She was at the dinner the other night. I resisted a detour to her table, but a lot of good that did me! She's quite a lady, elegant yet tempered with an open warmth, and that voice of hers, so rich and liquid.'

'She's English; the women voters mightn't like it.'

'What about the special relationship?'

'Yeah!' Johnson reacted cynically.

'This one-to-one I've promised...'

'Back off, for God's sake. The one-to-one's big trouble!'

'I gave my word, Joss.'

'I'll square it.'

'No, my friend, I'm not heading for the burrow like a frightened rabbit: no way!'

'This whole thing could damage us!'

'How badly?'

'Badly, Sir!'

'My friend Sir James Babbington is due shortly: we'll hang the reason for the one-to-one on that.'

'But Mr President...'

'That's it, Joss!'

*

Joss Johnson wasn't happy. His boss was casting months of patient work aside. But there was nothing he could do, for when

John Duncan said 'That's it' there was no turning back. Of course, the nation might applaud the thought of a romance. That was a possibility, but in an election year it was high risk.

Johnson walked slowly back to his office. Someone was behind this girlfriend rumour. It wasn't just an energetic journalist. The editor, if not the owners of the newspaper, had given their approval. Suddenly he had the thought to scan the guest list for the recent dinner. He had the disk. Johnson quickened pace.

It was almost the first name he saw, JP Sebbson, the super-rich tycoon and his guest, newspaper boss Jake Crystal. Surprise, surprise, it was a Crystal Corporation newspaper that had carried the girlfriend story. There was no proof, of course, but the smoke signals seemed more than just coincidence. Joss smiled; he'd been invited to a press reception that was in two days' time. Almost certainly Crystal would be there. Joss Johnson's smile retreated. Crystal was a cautious creature, furtive almost in his manner and not a man to welcome questions. He was thin of body and of face, the very opposite of his bumptious friend, the so-called toast of Wall Street, JP Sebbson, or Seb as he was 'affectionately' known, but not by Joss, who saw him as a ruthless SOB who'd sell his mother for a dime and probably had!

Joss sat down wearily behind his office desk. 'Best deal with the one-to-one thing right now,' he muttered with a feeling of resigned resolution. He lifted the phone. He smiled; it just was like passing John's note to his girl friend at college; indeed, something he had done.

'Sarah Crawford.' The President was right. Her voice was something else.

'It's Joss Johnson, and I don't know what to say, quite honestly, other than to tell you that the one-to-one's still on. He wants to hang it on the imminent arrival of your Prime Minister. I'm sorry you've become an election pawn, but there it is.'

'Joss, I know the media game and I don't mind withdrawing from the interview, if that would help the President.'

'He won't hear of it. I know the signs. He's got the bit between his teeth. Now he may phone you himself but I thought I'd give you a little prior warning. And, Sarah, if you need any help don't hesitate to lift the phone. The FBI is watching but we're not using the police, for that makes it look too official and would help the rumourmongers. Remember, if things get rough, you could always stay with Joan and me.'

'Joss, you're being really kind, but I think I'll tough it out for a while. Thanks again and, Joss, hanging the one-to-one on the PM's visit is perfect.'

'The President doesn't know about this call, but I'll fill him in. Bye, Sarah.'

'Bye.'

*

Sarah's phone was busy and, even though her number wasn't listed, the cranks got through. Some of it was pretty crude. Indeed, the last call had been particularly nasty. It was time to unplug but just as her hand stretched out to disconnect, the phone rang out again.

'All right,' she said aloud. 'Just one more.'

'John Duncan here.'

'Not another crank.'

'No, not another one, the real crank, Sarah!'

'Mr President, I'm sorry but... it's been... Oh heavens, I've mislaid my PR image!'

Duncan laughed.

'Sarah, I'm sorry you've been subject to the dirty tricks brigade. Joss spoke to you earlier and offered to put you up. The offer still holds, he says.'

'Well, Sir, after this morning's bombardment, I think it would be prudent to accept.'

'Good, that's done. Now, Sarah, the one-to-one: because of the current fuss and seemingly unbounded interest, this event will draw the viewers by the million. We need to book prime time a week before Sir James arrives, so I have two weeks to get my act together. We will also need to give you some leads etc, but as you'll be staying with Joss, I'm sure we can arrange something. Is that OK?'

'I'm just a bit overwhelmed, Sir, I'll need a little time.'

'Sarah, being overwhelmed at the White House is the daily menu! My secretary's making signs – my next caller. We'll speak soon.'

'Thank you, Mr President.'

She sat down; the world seemed to be revolving like the circling platform of her microwave. She had wanted a one-to-one and, by heavens, this was it: prime time, prime interest. This would test her so-called calm unflappability!

*

Chapter Nine

The President had asked Harry Roberts to sit in on his weekly economic briefing. Here trends were outlined and discussed and those who knew the current systems quoted in-house economic jargon liberally. Most of it left Harry totally baffled. Nothing was simple; indeed, they seemed to love the endless complication, swinging from the macro to the micro view with careless ease.

This particular morning there was an undisguised battle between the opposing theories held by two of the youngest advisors, concerning the Federal Reserve's attitude to rising interest rates. The President's frustration was obvious but he didn't let it master him.

'Gentlemen, if this is what's on offer, it's little wonder that economics has been called the dismal science. I'm not saying that what you've been discussing isn't relevant. Far from it, for our complicated world demands it. As Eliot said, "We are distracted from distraction by distraction," and it's a wonder that we stumble through the maze so well.

'Well, folks, I'm an awkward cuss. I don't believe this drab picture of economics. I believe it is the science of opportunity and a science that, if properly pursued, can emancipate humanity. I would appreciate your reflections at our next gathering. Thank you.'

The economists filed out, leaving the President and Harry alone in the Oval Office. For a long time the President said nothing, then he chuckled.

'Harry, I hope you noticed I took your advice; I didn't breathe a word of Henry George!'

'The time will come. Now, we need new words to say the old eternal things!'

'Harry, I like it – "new words to say the old eternal things" – brilliant! That's it in a nutshell!'

They sat quietly for a time.

'That thing you do, being aware of the body on the chair and connecting with the listening; I've been doing it and I find it very useful. And paying attention to the little things like lifting up a pen: I remember one of those hostages who were held for months somewhere in the Lebanon. After his release he found that walking to the car was just as big a deal as driving it. Indeed, after being incarcerated for so long every little act was precious. No moment was a throwaway!'

'Nicely put, Sir: yes, every moment is the present moment and it's the only time we know.' Harry laughed. 'I suppose, Sir, you could say tomorrow never comes until it is today!'

The President chuckled as he relaxed further into the sofa and its cushions.

'Harry, from today you're on my personal staff. I'm only making official what's already happened.'

'Thank you, Sir.'

The President remained reflective.

'This one-to-one with Sarah Crawford will have wall-to-wall coverage, as the gossip element will make the viewing figures astronomic.'

'I know, the press can't leave it alone. It's the perfect front page story and, Sir, she is impressive.'

'Yes, Harry, she is. The truth is I like her, but I feel constrained. Joss is in election mode and I feel obliged to toe the line.'

Pointedly Harry didn't respond.

'You're very quiet, my friend.'

'Well, Sir, in my book elections shouldn't come into it.'

The President nodded.

'Now this one-to-one: we'll need to burn the midnight oil. I want ideas that people can relate to. As you just said a moment ago; "new words to say the old eternal things."'

'How dare we tolerate the scourge of poverty! This is a moral question, Mr President and until it's viewed like this I doubt that much will happen.'

The President nodded. Harry was right: it was a moral question. This clearly was the keystone and it would stir the nation more than all the fancy figures from the Fed Reserve.

The phone rang.

'Right,' was the President's brief response.

'The French Ambassador has arrived downstairs. So, that's it for today.'

*

Harry acknowledged the secretaries as he passed through the adjoining office. Trying to look important was not on his agenda. Anyway, the powerful ex-Marine was naturally impressive and his ready smile made him popular, especially with the President's secretary.

Being deep in thought, he almost bumped into Joss Johnson.

'Brainstorming with the President again,' Joss quipped.

'Not much of a storm with this brain, Mr Johnson.'

'That's not what I hear, and, by the way, it's Joss! Would it be convenient to attend the staff meeting tomorrow morning? My secretary will give you the details.'

Harry mumbled 'yes'. He was too bewildered to say much else

'You'll have a desk, of course, but you'll have to share with one of the other fellas.'

'Thank you, Sir.' For Harry, using 'Joss' was much too premature.

Joss Johnson rushed off, leaving Harry even more bewildered. Obviously the President had spoken and the wheels were now in motion. Such was the power of patronage. The truth was that, without his rapport with the President, he would still be driving limos, not that that was onerous, indeed, he rather liked the job, and driving the President was not routine.

He needed ideas. This was his discussion group night but he couldn't tell them anything even though they were his trusted friends. He dared not compromise the President. Harry was well aware of the down side of his situation. He was the man whispering in the President's ear and could be seen as a Rasputin if the second term was threatened by John Duncan's thrust for change. The friendly White House staff could turn on him and hang him out to dry.

He walked on down the corridor, nodding to familiar people whose name he didn't know. He wasn't an insider. In fact, he was the President's man, united, not politically, but by an understanding of the deeper things of life and shared experience.

Chapter Ten

JP Sebbson wiped his forehead with the hotel's generous serviette and sat back on the well-upholstered chair.

'Jake, how do you keep so goddam cool?'

'There's nothing of me, Seb, and Seb, it's the Fall not Summer!'

'Yeah,' Sebbson muttered, while finishing off the fish course.

'I'm worried, Jake. Duncan's cottoned on to real estate!'

'Jeez, who hasn't? It's the biggest money spinner there is.'

'Yeah, but Duncan wants to put his sticky paws on it.'

'Cheer him on, Seb, he'll never get past Congress. Those guys know what side their toast is buttered on! Anyway, there's been nothing reported and the media have been silent. So what's the big deal?'

'I've someone on the inside, a young economist who visits the White House. He tells me that there's a guy who sits in on meetings but says nothing. I put the private dicks on to this and guess what: this fella belongs to a group who studies philosophy and the economics of Henry George. So you get my drift.'

'Seb, it's a free country, we can study what we like. But putting theories into practice is a different ball game. Cool it and enjoy the meal, for crissake!'

'This is different, Jake. Duncan can swing the crowd. I've watched him. He could return with a landslide and a mandate. The Dow Jones would free fall!'

'That would stop him, then! Jeez, you are worked up!'

'I sure am. This site tax thing these Georgists rabbit on about is dynamite!'

'Seb, I'm usually the worrier, but after a glass of decent white I mellow. Drink up! Dammit, George's ideas have been around for a hundred years and with all their talk it's come to virtually nothing. Why should Duncan spring the rabbit? This obsession of yours is goddam unhealthy!'

'Listen, Jake, that fella across the square from where we're eating...'

'Good old Lafayette Square,' Crystal interjected.

'Yeah, that fella's got it. Duncan knows the secret!'

'Seb, that wine you chose is good, but I didn't know it was *that* good. "Secret" – what do you mean for crissake? What *secret*?'

'Real estate location value belongs to the community and guys like us have been stealing it for years!'

'Yeah, from George and Martha's time! Jeez, wise up, Seb!'

'Duncan will make this a moral crusade. I goddam know it!'

'Seb, you need a shrink! But in the meantime let's freshen up your glass.'

They both savoured another mouthful.

'Tell me, Seb, why will Duncan make it a moral issue?

'Because the private claiming of location value is a major cause of poverty!'

'Idleness is the cause of poverty. Any fella with some go in him can make it!'

'Jake, that's real easy to say but only very few can cross the track. Take Manhattan, not even a bastard like me would claim that he created the value of his real estate!'

'You built the scrapers!'

'They're just buildings. It's the location that matters and that location value by right and reason belongs to the community. But real estate law allows private interest to claim the community's location value and the community in turn plunders wages, not real estate. So the rich get richer and the poor, having little or no real estate, struggle on, or lose out. It's inevitable!'

'I got it, Seb, but that wouldn't go down too well round the table at TO Trading!'

'You bet!'

Jake filled the glasses once again. Old fire-eating Seb was having a crisis of conscience. It was hard to believe, but maybe when the wine wore off he'd slither back to normal. Meanwhile, Jake decided not to push it; the old calculating caution was still hovering. Seb, he knew, could lash out all too easily; it was best not to provoke him further.

Jake Crystal was concerned for his old friend Seb. He had acted very strangely, for normally he was crowing over some new acquisition or how he'd asset stripped some crumbling corporation. Seb could be a selfish bastard but he had a good side, for Jake remembered when he'd lost his wife, Seb turned up often on the doorstep.

The first thing Crystal did when returning to his corporate office was to see his chief accountant, who, as well as accountancy, had majored in economics.

'Al, what do you know of an economist called George?'

'Henry George – he was influential at the end of the nineteenth and beginning of the twentieth century. His big thing was site value. But nobody reads him now; he's way beyond his sell-by date.'

'Have you read him?'

'Bits and pieces.'

'Don't bullshit me, Al. How can you tell me that he's past his sell-by date, if you haven't read his stuff!' Crystal's sharp eyes cut like lasers. 'I don't want the prejudice of some slick lecturer, I want your own opinion, OK! Take time to read his book and let me know. It's urgent. See me before lunch tomorrow at the latest!'

Crystal's darting eyes seemed to pick up everything and, as with most of the staff, they always made him feel uneasy.

'It's a long book, Sir.' Al ventured tentatively.

'Do your best, Al', Crystal replied quietly. Al had never heard that sound before.

Jake was meeting Seb again to morrow evening. They were seeing two big hitters at Seb's club. Media guys whose spreading wings were stretching far and wide. Too wide, Jake thought. He had seen it often; guys puffed with swollen egos flying way above the safety level. The trouble was if Seb was not his usual razor-sharp incisive self he could make some silly moves. Indeed, the more Jake thought of it, the more he was concerned. Seb's lunchtime mood had been most odd. Henry George, he mused. Maybe he ought to read his goddam book as well.

*

Chapter Eleven

Sarah now knew the sharp end of media intrusion from the other side. Long-focus lenses followed her journeys to the studio and her various appointments. The FBI did their best but the interest was insatiable. The sensible thing, of course, was to fly back to Britain, but with the one-to-one and the PM's visit to Camp David, that was not an option. So she had to stick it out. There was another reservation, something she was slow to acknowledge even to herself: her growing liking for John Duncan. Indeed, when reporting home, her BBC impartiality was often close to being breached.

The truth was she had been naturally attracted to him on the evening of the White House dinner. But she hadn't let her feelings run amok. People were attracted to people, and there the matter often rested. However, the endless speculation linking them romantically brought a measure of reality and, of course, the human mind was good at painting pictures.

Joss had filled her in on all the eccentricities of the White House but she wanted to see the actual setting of the interview. The President had also indicated that some preliminary words regarding what he hoped to say might help her preparation. They were due to meet and, contrary to her usual professional calm, she felt ill at ease, almost girlish in her agitation.

Two days later, when they did meet, she felt nervous, but this soon gave way to simple awkwardness, as the unspoken language that flashed between them was all too obvious. Indeed, their mutual attraction was reality. Even so, nothing was said as the President escorted her through the outer area where the secretaries, discreetly busy, curbed their curiosity. The door opened and she was in the Oval Office.

'Here, I think,' Duncan said briefly, indicating two easy chairs.

'That would be fine, Sir.'

'I plan to introduce a new direction in this administration's policy. So, Sarah, I may be controversial here and there.' He smiled. 'Poor old Joss is having nightmares about poll ratings!'

'Would it be useful for me to have some prior notice of the issues?' Sarah asked tentatively, sensing the President's underlying strength. John Duncan was bright and the energy reflected in his eyes confirmed it. He had well-formed features, though on the rugged side. He certainly wasn't a smoothie.

They sat down on the chairs the President had selected for the one-to-one.

'First of all I'll be saying quite a lot about the unanimity that unites Britain and America on many foreign policy matters. On this Sir James and I, with our various teams, will have a working week-end at Camp David, as you know.' Duncan laughed. 'You, of course, will be asking the questions and will largely influence the direction of the interview, but Sarah I'm a stubborn cuss and will end up saying what I want!

'There are the Americas and the relationship between our two continents and, of course, there is the commercial and economic scene. Is there a moral dimension to our world-wide corporate activity? Is there a moral dimension to the way we fund the state? Is there an equitable balance between nature's laws and human behaviour? These questions have arisen and grown persistent since my sojourn in the Mall, but this is off the record.'

'Searching questions, Sir,' Sarah responded, her voice still tentative.

John Duncan was aware of the tentative note; it spoke of vulnerability, and warmth rose naturally for this graceful lady whom he'd met once socially. She was certainly attractive. He had seen her on TV and with the journalists at the briefings, but the dinner party was the first occasion he'd enjoyed her company. She had an almost classical look and, of course, her voice... well, that English tone was captivating.

Duncan stretched his feet out in front of him. Lost for words, he simply rested, waiting for a prompt of inspiration. When it came it sounded very ordinary.

'I'm sorry you've been harassed by this media thing, but having dinner with the President can have some serious side-effects! I must say, I've been rather flattered by it all. I'm told my polls are up, so the voters clearly think I have some taste!'

Sarah laughed but the embarrassed note was obvious.

'Being a voting asset is a first for me, Mr President!'

The President chuckled, while punching out his secretary's number.

'Mary, has Harry arrived?'

'Yes, Sir.' The sound was on audio.

'Send him in, and could you rustle up four coffees?'

'Yes, Sir.'

There was a knock and the ex-Marine filled the doorway.

'Harry,' the President called, 'meet Sarah Crawford.'

'So this is where you've been hiding Miss Crawford, Mr President.'

'Yes, Harry, I even fooled the FBI.'

'That's easy, Sir, CNN's the problem!' Harry was gaining in confidence.

They all laughed and Duncan was pleased to see that Sarah was no longer ill at ease.

'Mr Roberts, I've been hearing about you from Mr Johnson. He tells me that you have a gift for words.'

'Ma-am, he must be thinking of some other fella!'

There was another burst of laughter just as Mary entered with the coffee. Puzzled, she scanned the room.

'I'm sorry, Sir, I thought you asked for four coffees.'

'I did. One's for *you!* You've been here from early morning. It's time you stopped!'

Again they laughed.

'Well, Harry, what have you discovered? Have you any more gems?'

'Gems don't turn up to order, Sir, '

'Exactly, they reveal themselves, we have to wait.' The President smiled. 'So what has been revealed?'

Harry chuckled.

'Well, Sir, you have been emphasising the moral dimension...'

'Yeah, I've been banging on about it!'

'I looked up the word "moral" in the dictionary and it talked about the difference between right and wrong. And then I picked up another book outlining the history of modern philosophers and was completely confused. Hume and Kant and co are not exactly easy, and moral relativism completely floored me. But, Sir, when you mention the moral dimension in your speeches the people don't run to their dictionaries. They know what you're on about, even the guys who sneer and think it's just for prudes. So my question is this: is moral motivation natural to the human being?'

The President grinned.

'Sarah, you studied philosophy at university, I believe'

'That is what my piece of paper says, but answering questions such as Mr Roberts poses is another matter. I have a further question, though. If human beings show no sign of moral sensitivity, are they human? Is morality an in-built requirement of humanity, and if it's absent will society suffer and eventually collapse?'

'I would answer yes, but as Joss would ask, would it pull the votes?'

'Your words would need to touch a chord of recognition,' Sarah returned.

'There you are, Harry, "We need new words to say the old eternal things!"'

'Well put, Mr President,' Sarah reacted.

'Harry's words, Sarah. I'm his PR man!'

Sarah's laughter was delightful and Duncan was captivated.

'So Mr Johnson was right!' Sarah quipped.

'He's rarely wrong.'

There was a pause in the conversation while they all sipped their coffee.

'Good coffee, Mary.'

'We aim to please, Mr President.'

Sarah was feeling happy and wholly relaxed. This was good company.

'Mr President, you mentioned the moral dimension in relation to funding the state. I can't quite see the connection, Sir.'

'I'll put it bluntly, Sarah. Is it moral for the state to plunder the earnings of the citizen?'

'Certainly not, Sir.'

'And is it moral for the individual, or a corporate group, to steal the rightful revenue of the community?'

'Again, Sir, no!'

'Well, that's exactly what's happening, albeit with the full backing of the law. It's the economics of the madhouse, but the madhouse has been up and running for some time. No one can imagine anything better. Of course, some don't want it any better, for they're doing pretty well by playing the system. It's the way the mind-set is and few see past it.'

'Sorry, Mr President, but I'm clearly missing something.'

'My apologies, I've been guilty of assumptions. Let's take the Manhattan skyline, which obviously reflects enormous wealth. Who created that wealth?'

'The developers, the corporate groups, I suppose. There are a host of factors.'

'True, but would these developers and corporate groups have risked their capital on a location of equal size in, say, the plains of South Dakota, or the Alaskan north?'

'Hardly, Sir, there'd be little point in building a ghost town, even if the land were cheap!'

'Yet they scramble like beggars for a site in Wall Street. Location matters, it would seem. Now to return to the question: who creates the location value?'

'It's difficult to single anyone out. It's the collective presence of... well, everybody.'

'Exactly, Sarah, the community as a whole creates the location value, but real estate law allows individuals and corporate groups to claim it, or, as I rather bluntly said, steal the rightful revenue of the community.'

'Good heavens, and the state plunders our salaries and calls it income tax! This is dynamite. Why has no one ever mentioned this?'

'Vested interests, Sarah: some would have a lot to lose. Then there's patchwork suburbia. Opposition doesn't have to be invented!'

The phone rang. It was still on audio but the President let it be.

'Mr Anderson for you, Mr President.'

'Where is it this time Andy?'

'The Balkans are hotting up again.'

'And the EU?'

'Talking!'

'I'll put a call through to Sir James. Thanks, Andy, let's keep close on this one. Bye.'

'Sorry, there's more. There's trouble from some extremist group in the Lebanon, but we're hoping that, with the cooperation of Syria, it'll be contained. There's been more rioting in Pakistan, stirred up by the "fundos", in other words the fundamentalists.'

'Andy, make sure our personnel take no foolhardy risks. We don't want another hostage crisis. Anything else?'

'Agrarian protests somewhere in South America – one of the big states, I believe. It's only coming in.'

'Land reform, Andy, land reform, it's overdue. Keep in touch, OK. Have a good evening.'

'That was a modest list,' the President quipped. 'The trouble is that any one of those incidents could flare up all too easily and, of course, someone's bound to point the finger in our direction.'

The President stood up.

'This has been a most enjoyable session. Unfortunately, I'm due at a dinner in an hour's time. Harry, we'll talk tomorrow and, Sarah, Joss is taking you home, I believe. I'll escort you to his office.'

Chapter Twelve

He could have dismissed it easily; indeed, before his experience on the morning of his walk-about, he would have done so. It was very brief, but this figure walked across the room and it was he, himself, yet wholly unfamiliar. He felt unable to share the experience with anyone as the whispered rumour that 'he's being strange again' could easily spread, especially with the memory of his 'disappearance.' Even Joss might take it wrongly. Harry, it seemed, was the only sympathetic ear.

In the event Harry was almost casual.

'Oh, that's your personality, Sir. When it's not being powered it's as lifeless as a jacket.'

'And when it's powered?'

'We believe it's us! I had one or two similar happenings in the Gulf.'

'You've never talked much about your time over there.'

'No, Sir, I used to get nightmares but they've almost gone. Some guys hit the bottle and I don't blame them, but I was lucky. Just met the right fella at the right time.'

'Then, Harry, who am I, if I'm not this clutch of feelings called John Duncan?'

'That's the big one, Sir.'

'Listen, I'm late for the Joint Chiefs. Indeed, there never seems to be enough time. Let's have supper one evening and if you think Mary would appreciate our eccentric conversation, bring her along. I'm very glad you two are walking out, to use the good old-fashioned term. Good news!'

'Thank you, Mr President.'

Harry closed the door gently behind him as he left. For such a big man his movements were quiet and careful. Perhaps he was putting into practice what he'd learned at his group. The Oval Office was suddenly quiet and the President alone. He had the choice, it seemed, to sense the presence or to feel the pain of loneliness, which now was prompted by the thought of Sarah Crawford.

*

Jake Crystal was pleased to note that his friend JP Sebbson had slithered back to something like normality. His attraction to the corporate game had won, banishing the inconvenient shafts of reformation. Yet he hadn't quite recovered, for his ruthlessness had lost its sharp unheeding edge. Something had shifted. He had ignored Joe Smolensky, known for his strong-arm tactics and also known for his anti-Duncan stance. Duncan was a 'goddam red', and the 'enemy of business', Smolensky grated loudly. Normally Seb would have cheered him on and slapped him on the back, but not this time. This time he turned away, even though there was a growing anti-Duncan lobby. Still, Jake was careful not to bring the subject up. In this Jake's traditional caution won. Seb would spill the beans in time. Jake suspected that his old friend was playing a long game but what that was, was known to God and Seb alone.

'Senator, Sebbson's gone off the boil. I haven't heard a word for days,' Ed Vince called out as he rushed noisily into Whitehead's office.

'Thank God for that.'

'Well, Sir, his cash is useful.'

'We'll get by.'

'Yeah, you're right! That tycoon Smolensky phoned...'

'Ed, back off. That guy's bad news. He's mafia!'

'He said all the right things.'

'Those fellas always do. Ed, we're out in front and Smolensky senses a winner, so he's hedging his bets. I wouldn't trust him with the morning coffee!

'Yeah, he keeps bad company. The fuss about this Crawford dame hasn't made much difference to the polls.'

'If the President's got a girlfriend, that's his affair. We're fighting this campaign on issues – period.'

'Issues, yeah, OK, but the press won't play the Nice Guy game!'

'That applies to us, as well as the President – it's issues, Ed. We need to rekindle the frontier spirit in this country. We're sliding into a dependence culture just like Europe. We need vigour, covered-wagon vigour, Ed, not PC vigilantes telling us what to think and how to think it!'

'I like it!' Ed enthused.

Ed was like a weather-vane, changing with the latest rush of air. His enthusiasms bubbled endlessly but he seemed incapable of holding a direction. The trouble was he lacked plain common sense. Imagine buttering up that crocodile Smolensky. Sam Whitehead had made his decision. Ed would have to be replaced and with no little tact. He would still keep his title but he'd be 'assisted' by a strategy expert, and that expert would be Whitehead's cousin. However Ed's emotions could flash volcanic at the hint of any slight. There was a real prospect of disruption in the camp, but Ed could not continue like the prototype loose cannon. God, why had he employed him in the first place?

'Smolensky! Jeez, God knows what Ed had said to him!'

Smolensky had been a boxer in his early years and his face confirmed it. He'd come up the hard way. Yet he could be charming, and oozed it when the need arose. His conglomerate was ever eager to expand, reflecting Joe Smolensky's obsessive ambition. Real estate being the prize, he was known to asset strip perfectly viable companies. He was ruthless, yet always sounded plausible when interviewed. His wealth was proverbial, but he had a past, and his ever-present guards tended to betray it.

His fellow tycoon Sebbson had ignored him at the last gathering. Joe put it down to jealousy. Seb was a big hitter and, like Joe himself, sensitive to rivals. Strange though, for Seb had always shown him an affable side. Joe was puzzled; maybe unknowingly he had trampled on some deal or other.

Joe was ever active. Now it was the Presidential front-runner. Vince was his contact: a bit of a boy scout, but useful. Joe always kept his options open. But Duncan was a closed book. He'd tried, but failed to penetrate the magic circle.

Chapter Thirteen

Four days before the scheduled one-to-one, news broke that members of an Anglo-American fact finding mission had been abducted in the Gulf area of the Middle East. The press, of course, were demanding action, but such emotional outpourings had little relevance to the hard realities on the ground. To John Duncan it was all too predictable, but nothing happened. There was no video, and no demands by the captors. This was strange, as the kidnap of six well-informed officials was top-line publicity. Were they *jihadists* or were they simply criminals? No one knew. Was it some new ultra-fundo group who'd been embarrassed by success and therefore lacked the proper back-up?

For an incumbent President seeking a second term the news was most disturbing. The captors would know this, and doubtless they would spin it out, hoping that a desperate President, with his ratings falling, would give in to pressure. In the meantime all the most powerful nation in the world could do was wait. Intelligence forces would be busy, of course, but penetrating the tribal loyalties of the Middle East wasn't easy.

President Duncan was in contact with the British PM, Sir James Babbington, daily. The Brits were digging away but no one claimed to have an easy answer.

The day of the one-to-one had at last arrived. It was shadowed by the hostage crisis but by no means overshadowed. In some ways the public had been anesthetized by horror from that quarter. And, of course, the enormous build-up of interest fed by front-page coverage had fostered curiosity. With so much anticipation hanging on the event, the danger of anticlimax was all too real.

Sarah was nervous but she covered it well; anyway, the countdown period was always difficult. The President took his seat with ten minutes to spare. He'd been on the phone to Sir James Babbington, he told Sarah, and if he was on edge he didn't show it.

The make-up people fussed and Duncan suffered their attentions stoically. At last they were given the signal. It had been arranged that the President should begin with a brief statement on the hostage situation and this he did, saying that, in conjunction with the British Prime Minister, all avenues of enquiry were being pursued.

'For the families involved this is a nightmare, and our sympathy goes out to them. Be assured, though, that all will be done that can be done. I must say that the cooperation of the Gulf States has been generous and unreserved. So let's pray that, with God's help, this dreadful situation will be resolved quickly.'

He turned to Sarah and nodded gently.

'Now, Sarah, you're in charge.'

Sarah Crawford began by echoing the President's sentiments on the hostage situation and by thanking the President for granting her the honour of the one-to one. Her early nervousness had eased. Indeed, it was the usual experience when an interview got under way.

Her questions focused firstly on the coming summit at Camp David, and these the President answered with fluent ease.

'I know, Mr President, that you and Sir James are friends and that you consult often. Can I therefore assume that 'the special relationship' is still special?'

Duncan laughed.

'One thing about families, Sarah, is their propensity for plain speaking, yet despite this, they almost always come together at Christmas. The bond is strong and a disagreement now and then lends honesty and makes the bonding more resilient.'

'In the recent weeks you have often emphasized the need for morality in commerce at home and in the global sphere. But, Mr President, fierce competition and established custom in many developing countries makes exploitation all too easy. How can this be overcome?'

'With difficulty: for tampering with the market is always fraught with unexpected problems. Even so, goodwill is a powerful force and example is its most convincing ally. We must at least be willing to try. Few thought that the slave trade could be ended, but Wilberforce persisted and in the end he won the day. Morality, I believe, is natural to the human. We simply need reminding of our better parts, instead of wallowing in inactive cynicism! When a practice is wrong it is wrong and as a civilized society we should move to change it. Now, there is plenty in our nation that is plainly wrong. How can we tolerate the poverty that we see around us? How dare we tolerate it! Words of regret are little more than glib complacency unless we turn our minds to real reform. Here I'm not speaking of charity, which, alas, is often all too necessary. No, I'm speaking of justice. Give the people justice. We have civil justice. Now it's time to turn our minds to economic justice. In a nation such as ours, there is enough for all and plenty'.

'These are inspiring aspirations, Mr President, but many will be sceptical and view your words as merely rhetoric! Or do I hear the socialist drum beat?'

'Far from it! In my opinion Socialism does not suit this country. Here I agree with Senator Whitehead, the Republican front-runner. We need and understand the frontier spirit, but such thrusting enterprise should not be free to run amok like some unfettered warlord culture. It needs the bridle of the law that is both just and natural. Justice is the key to economic stability and progress. It also is a moral duty, for here lies the answer to the curse of poverty.'

'Mr President, what is the answer?'

Duncan laughed.

'That is for the next one-to-one! Sarah, nature doesn't have a right-wing or a leftist agenda. Her rule is natural and we need to find and understand her laws. One question I would leave with all those who are watching. What is location value? And the supplementary - Who created it? And if you want another – To whom does it belong? This enquiry is a matter for us all!'

Joss Johnson, who was watching in his office, was appalled.

'Jeez, he's just lost the election,' he whispered. But Harry Roberts, who was watching with him, took a different line.

'He wants the people to see for themselves. It's good!'

The questions were now focused on South America, and here the President was deftly sensitive. Praising the good parts was his careful approach.

The time was almost up and Sarah asked the President if he had any closing comments.

'Just to thank you for your courtesy and to hope another one-to-one will be forthcoming. Finally, though, let us remember the plight of the hostages and pray for their safe and speedy return.'

'Thank you, Mr President.'

*

A flurry of activity soon cleared the Oval Office of all broadcasting equipment and personnel, leaving Sarah and the President still talking amiably.

'Now, Sarah, you're got media savvy. What about tomorrow's headlines?'

'Mixed. It's a difficult one to call, for your speech invited reflection not reaction. There will be reaction, of course, and pretty violent, I would say, for pointing out the truth the way you did can stir the hornets' nest. Your questions, though, could end up front page and in heavy type.'

'That's exactly what I want!'

Chapter Fourteen

'*Question Time,*' 'Three Questions,' 'President hands out Homework,' were three brief but neutral headlines. 'Quit moralizing Mr President; *you* give us answers!' was clearly in the 'anti' camp, but most followed a plain reporting line, such as 'President poses questions.' The more popular tabloid papers concentrated on the human story of Sarah Crawford and the President. One headline ran, 'The BBC's "First Lady"' – 'First Lady' was in bold type. One business-oriented newspaper accused the President of dangerous meddling. 'Don't upset the markets Mr President' was the message.

The hostage crisis was still on the front page but as the captors had not revealed themselves or made demands there was little to say. The first interviews with the families were emerging. These were emotional and written up, as it were, by the reporters. But the families themselves made no criticisms.

The President had fared better than Joss Johnson had expected but he knew the dangers weren't past. The political and economic gurus were yet to show their wares and they, he guessed, would be mostly negative. They wouldn't like their cosy world upset by economic illiterates, even if he were the President. As for the hostage situation, Joss was a realist. Blame would eventually fasten on the President, if no solution were forthcoming. Reason didn't figure.

He found his friend the President unusually fascinated by the papers.

'Joss, most of them have focused on the questions. I never thought I'd be so lucky, for it's exactly what I wanted.'

'I wish *I* knew what you wanted. It's very early days, Mr President, for when the Wall Street experts go to press, your second term could be a no-fly zone!'

'I wonder. Your fears are well grounded, Joss, but truth is a strange animal. People can change course, and allies appear in the most unexpected quarter.'

'Mr President, we're old friends, old college pals, so we know each other well, but in the last weeks you've changed. Somehow you're not thinking politically, and it unnerves me. You're going for the big one, and there's part of me that likes it, but the other part is worried that you're throwing everything away, and I'm sorry if I say it, almost carelessly.'

'Joss, why don't you forget this Mr President thing for a while? You know, when we're alone like this.'

'You've said this before, Sir.' Joss shook his head. 'It wouldn't feel right. Anyway, the formality reminds me that I'm serving more than the person.'

'OK. So be it. Now, Joss, your concern that I'm throwing all our hard-won gains away. I understand what you're saying and in some ways I agree, but, Joss, I'm following an instinct. It's as if my script's been written for me. It's a strange feeling, but there it is. And, Joss, I'm not crazy. In fact, I feel the opposite, like a fine energy. Some might call it excitement, but it's not that. It's early days. Let's see how this spins out.' Duncan smiled, looking quizzically at his Chief of Staff. 'Are you with me on this wagon or are you clambering to get out?'

'I'm tightening my seat belt, Sir!'

'That's Joss!'

*

When Harry Roberts saw Joss returning to his office, he went to see him.

'Does the President want to see me, Sir?'

'Yes, Harry, the usual. Hey, isn't it time you called me Joss? Everybody does!'

'It wouldn't seem right, Mr Johnson.'

'You're one of the old school, Harry. Well, that's no bad thing, but maybe in a year or so when we get to know each other?'

Both men burst out laughing.

'He's in the Oval Office,' Joss said easily as Harry left. He liked Harry. The big man wasn't troubled with ambition. Indeed, any resentment Joss had entertained at Harry's popularity with the President had disappeared, for the ex-Marine was totally unassuming.

The President was on the phone when Harry knocked and

entered. Harry waited.

'That was the Secretary of State. Not a squeak from these guys in the Gulf.'

'Sounds like a new lot, Sir, who haven't got their act together.'

'Or maybe they're winding up the drama. Jeez, the sum of human anxiety and distress...' The President didn't finish the sentence.

For a moment there was silence.

'What do you think of the headlines?'

'Good, Sir. I expected much more opposition.'

'Do you think I've been reckless, or perhaps a touch naïve?'

'Asking fundamental questions is not naïve, Sir, but being reckless is a feeling you would know yourself.'

'I seem to be waiting for the next stepping-stone to appear. It's a bit adventurous, but I wouldn't call it reckless. It's as though something knows the way and all we have to do is wait and then obey; but Harry, what knows?'

Harry smiled but made no answer.

'Harry, you're being coy!'

'Well, Sir – *you* know! But it's *you*, without the usual mental luggage.'

'A kind of Duncan, minus mind-set!'

They laughed.

'The British PM is coming next week for a session at Camp David. I would like you to be there. The President needs good men about him. Joss will be in the party and also the Secretary of State, Andy Anderson. It's fairly low key, for Jim Babbington and I don't stand on ceremony.'

'I'm greatly honoured, Sir.'

'You know, Harry, since that morning when the scales dropped briefly from my eyes, you're the only one that I can turn to, indeed, the only one that seems to understand. Doubtless there are gurus out there but, for the President, such forays would invite press trouble.

'You'll enjoy Camp David, especially with Jim as guest. The informal dinners can be fun. You can be the keeper of my questions! Are there natural laws that govern us in society, and if so what are they? Then there are the focused questions. What is location value? Who created it? And to whom does it belong?'

The President got up from his easy chair and stood poised for a moment.

'Mary will be with us, of course,' he said, smiling knowingly at Harry.

Harry, sensing something on the President's mind, kept silent.

'Sarah Crawford will be part of the British team,' Duncan said quietly, but he didn't look up or make any further comment and Harry was discreetly silent.

Still the President stood as if rooted to the spot.

'The hostages disappeared, Harry. They simply disappeared! There is no actual evidence that they were abducted, though it's near to certain that they were. We have no leads whatever and the American people will find that difficult to take!'

'Were there overheads at the time?'

'They must have checked that, Harry, but I'll confirm. Well, that's it. Andy Anderson's due any moment to discuss the prelims for Camp David.'

Chapter Fifteen

Andy Anderson was stuck in traffic at Dupont Circle and was running late. So, sitting back on his swivel chair, Duncan thought he'd practise Harry's exercise, but as the mind grew still he remembered Harry's question about the overheads. Acting on the impulse, he phoned the Defence Secretary.

'Hey, Rod, what info did we get from the fly-overs and the satellite coverage?'

'Nothing specific was reported. They would have checked, of course.'

'My sentiments, Rod, but could you check it out again? For, when you think of it, it's very odd that nothing was spotted. I was told that they had been travelling on the open road.'

'Yes, Sir, that was what they told us on their last call in.'

'Tell them to double check. OK, Rod?'

'Yes, Sir.'

Next Duncan punched Sarah Crawford's mobile number. He had been putting off the call like some embarrassed teenager.

'Sarah Crawford.' The voice was instant. It was as easy as that.

'John Duncan here, I'm just checking on your après one-to-one syndrome!'

'It's all right, Mr President, my knee-knocking rate is almost back to normal! The press have been much more gentle than I expected.'

'It's early days, Sarah. What about the British Press?'

'President savaged by Jane Austen' is one headline, I'm told.'

'And I've been in hospital since!'

Sarah's laughter flowed through the phone and Duncan was entranced.

There was a knock and the door edged open.

'Sorry, Sarah, Andy Anderson's just arrived. Be in touch.'

When Anderson left, the phone rang as if on cue. It was the

Defence Secretary, Rod Rosewell.

'Mr President, there's been an almighty mix-up. I could use other language but I know you are adverse to certain swearwords. There are images, which the experts say are army trucks, swarming like bees around a convoy, which they say is our lot. Langley thinks they're a rogue element of the Saudi army allied to some way-out Wahhabi element, but that's just guess-work, or, to be fair, an educated guess!'

'OK, I'll call in the Saudi Ambassador and do a little gentle probing. Thanks, Rod.'

Duncan put the phone down gently. 'Well, well, Harry Roberts, that's another bulls-eye' he whispered quietly.

Again John Duncan sat back hoping for a moment's quietness but that was tempting fate, he thought knowingly. The mind was a strange creature. Here he was undisturbed and quiet, yet the mind was busy waiting for the phone to ring like some mesmerised rabbit. Why not accept that it would ring when it would ring?

Then it did ring.

'The Prime Minister for you, Sir,' Mary intoned.

'Thanks, Mary.'

'John, the City over here thinks you're off your trolley!'

'They're slow on the uptake, Jim. I've been here for three years!'

'Seriously, John, this location value thing has set them chattering like fishwives. They say it's bloody mad to upset the property market.'

'Jim, these guys have their hands in the till and they know it!'

'John, the trouble is the whole damned pack of cards could tumble if you prod too much.'

'Jim, I'm prodding gently. Listen, we'll talk about this when you're over in the next few days. Is the good lady coming?'

'Wouldn't miss it.'

'She'll have Sarah Crawford to keep her company while we pontificate!'

'Good company, I would say.'

'You would be right.'

The two leaders continued to discuss mutual interest topics, ending with the hostage situation. Duncan confessed the overheads mix-up, but the PM was dismissive.

'John, cock-ups are the daily diet here at Number 10.'

'Well, Jim, we'll be meeting up soon.'

'All that's best until then.'

There were no long goodbyes when Jim was on the line, Duncan mused with a smile.

Once more he sat back, allowing stillness to grow. One minute, two, and then once more there was a buzz from Mary. His hand went out but there was no annoyance.

'Senator Whitehead wants to have a word with you. Shall I put him through?'

'Yes, of course, Mary.'

'Mr President, I hope I'm not intruding at an awkward time.'

'No, Senator, it's fine. What can I do for you?'

'Well, Sir, I overheard a conversation yesterday which disturbed me. I would like to get it off my chest, Sir, but I can't tell you over the phone. I need to see you, Mr President.'

'When would suit?'

'I'm at the Jefferson Hotel. I could be with you in not too many minutes.'

'What will we tell the press?'

'We could talk about the hostage crisis.'

'And we will. Good, see you in a few minutes.'

The phone went dead and Duncan pressed the buzzer, and almost immediately Mary appeared at the door.

'Where's Joss?'

'At the Hill, Sir,'

'And Harry?'

'In his office.'

'Ask him to escort Senator Whitehead upstairs. He'll be at the entrance in a few minutes.'

'Well, well,' Duncan whispered. 'Drama, indeed!'

Sam Whitehead was about the same size as Harry, but he, of course, was broader. They were both impressive men, Duncan thought, as they entered the Oval Office. Almost at once Harry took his leave and the Senator made a point of thanking him.

'A real pleasure to meet you, Mr Roberts.'

'Thank you, Senator.'

The door closed quietly, as always was the case with Harry. Almost immediately there was a knock.

'That's Mary with the coffee. Let's take these easy chairs.'

'Good coffee, Mr President,' Whitehead said with a kind of studied calm.

Duncan was amazed how 'the all-American boy' image fitted: definitely a handsome man.

'You may wonder why I've been so melodramatic. Well, here it is. Yesterday, I heard a whispered aside at a fund-raising dinner. The tone alerted me, for it was coldly sinister. In some strange way I heard it blind behind a pillar and the man in question wouldn't have suspected. The words were uncomplicated, but were like icicles. 'If Duncan dribbles on, I'll stop him, period, OK.' It kept me awake last night, Mr President, for the fella was Joe Smolensky and he's mafia!'

'Who was the other guy?'

'Sebbson.'

'Jeez!'

'Two ruthless SOB's!'

'Yeah, bastards, but with Sebbson it stops there,' Duncan said with certainty.

Whitehead laughed.

'I've never heard it put that way!'

'Well, Senator, I'm very grateful to you. Indeed, it confirms my already high opinion of your integrity. Now I'd better fill you in about the latest hostage situation. I'll get Harry in; he can be our witness in case the press get creative!'

He pressed Mary's number.

'Yes, Sir.' The audio was on.

'Ask Harry to come in and arm him with a coffee.'

'Yes, Mr President.'

'An impressive man, Sir. Roberts has a real sense of presence.'

Duncan readily agreed.

Harry duly arrived and, after twenty minutes of conversation, Whitehead suddenly threw up his hands.

'Why are we in opposition, for we think alike?'

'It's a game, Sam, and we have our roles!'

'I guess you're right. Well, Mr President, I should be going. Thank you for a most interesting half hour.'

'And thank you, Senator, for your earlier words.'

The Senator and Harry left and once again the President remembered the stillness. This time the phone didn't ring but Harry's gentle knock brought the practice to a close.

'A fine man' Sir,' was Harry's first comment.

'You're a clam, Harry, so I can tell you. He was warning me about Joe Smolensky, whose intentions may be less than benign.'

'Shall I get the security boys onto it?'

'Yes, Harry, but don't give Smolensky any cause for alarm. Why am I telling you this? For you know the game better than I do!'

Harry Roberts made no comment.

'You're quiet, Harry.'

'Well, Sir, you never know the whole game, for the bad guys play their first moves in the dark. After that the odds even up!'

'So, anticipating the first moves is the art.'

'Some spooks are very good at it.'

'And you met some?'

'Yeah,' Harry said briefly. 'Some real brave guys.'

Chapter Sixteen

Seb had slithered back towards his normal self but not as far as his old friend Jake Crystal had anticipated. Seb had grown to have respect for Duncan and this, for him, was something of a major shift, as in the recent past he'd ranted daily at the pinko President. Jake could only conclude that Seb's conscience had been recovered from cold storage, and defrosting was proceeding. What Jake hadn't noticed was that he himself was shifting in his point of view. Seb's company was having an effect.

What was very evident was the total breach with Joe Smolensky. Seb simply would have nothing to do with him when they met at corporate functions. The cold shoulder was very obvious.

Jake raised the subject at their usual luncheon date.

'Seb, you gave Joe Smolensky the big-time brush off last evening. That guy could turn real nasty!'

'Jake, take my advice, keep that bastard at arm's length. He wants the lot, the whole goddam cake. Nobody stands in his way and I mean *nobody!*'

'CEO's are rarely princes, Seb.'

'Yeah, but most draw the line somewhere. Jeez, even I do!' Seb smiled briefly.

Jake was again alerted, for Seb rarely joked about himself. Something was brewing but the brew had not matured. Jake had never pressed his prickly friend and he decided, as usual, to let Seb reveal himself in his own time. He almost always did.

Sarah felt anxious, miffed and generally agitated, as she'd heard nothing from the President since the one-to-one, except one ridiculously brief phone call. She was acting like a star-struck teenager. She chastised herself, but it made no difference. The restlessness persisted. Then two days before the PM's arrival date she received her marching orders. At least that was how she described her "it was hoped she would be able to" instructions to

Joss. She was to join a rather exclusive welcoming party at Andrews Air Force Base and would be whisked there in the Presidential helicopter. Her mind raced with speculation. 'So much for your even-minded maturity, my girl,' she muttered to herself

The party included the British Ambassador Roger Blackstone and his wife, the Secretary of State Andy Anderson and his lady, Sarah Crawford and, of course, the President. So, on the face of it, it seemed as if she were acting as the President's lady. On the other hand, she could be positioned with the Ambassador and his wife, thus making her part of the British contingent, which would be more appropriate. Indeed, as there would be the inevitable photographs, she was near to certain that that would be the line up, as standing with the President was the short cut to a press explosion.

*

The 'heavyweight' political and economic commentators were now penning their considered opinions and they were almost all of a negative nature. The President had asked the press office for the relevant cuttings and was busy scanning their content.

'Listen to this, Harry,' he called out. They were in the President's private office. Duncan was behind his desk and Harry was relaxing in the easy chair. 'Yeah, here's the passage. "Location value is just another way of saying land. This is an old idea fashionable a hundred ago. Its supporters were called *single taxers* and that exposes just how out of date the theory is. This is the Georgist message fashioned for the covered wagon age but not today." Here's another one. "Don't be fooled by this term *location value*, it's the land the IRS are after!" Now here's a piece of real invention. "Real Estate law protects the citizen from the greed of a rapacious state." Ah, and here we have the realist. "When you mix morality with economics you let the opposition in." Sounds like a line from the tycoon's charter!'

Harry chuckled.

'This is better than the evening chat show, Sir!'

'I know, I missed my calling!'

'Are there any positive comments?'

'Yes, a New York broadsheet. They say quite openly that location value is created by the community and by reason belongs to the community.'

'Whose the author, Sir?'

'Someone called Pucci.'
'Yes, he supports the Georgist line, but he's not well known.'
'Let's call him in.'
Roberts didn't respond.
'You've reservations, Harry.'
'Well, Mr President, I don't know the man personally but I've noticed that some Georgist fellas rant a bit and cause more harm than good.'
'We'll check him out. Harry, if St Francis came to visit us, we'd check him out!'
They laughed.
'Is there anything more you would like to say, Harry?'
'There is, Sir. Some commentators are equating location value with land tax. This is wrong. The land is given. It is the creator's gift and belongs to no one. What is collected is location value created by the community's presence. To repeat, the community collects what it has created.'
'The words reveal the man. We need more of this!'
They were silent for a time and stillness grew perceptibly. Neither looked for words to say or issues to debate. Indeed, the President had a growing trust that what was necessary would arise. This headless chicken running to and fro was such a waste of time.
'Harry,' Duncan said quietly, 'I would like your presence at Camp David. It will be a small party, that is, apart from the security boys.'
'This is quite an honour, Sir.'
'Don't worry, Harry, Mary will be there to hold your hand!'
Harry Roberts burst out laughing.

Chapter Seventeen

On the apron Sarah was placed with the British Ambassador and his wife. It was exactly as she had anticipated. She was well aware, of course, that such placings were irrelevant in the White House or indeed the helicopter.

The engine whine of the RAF jet had ceased. The portable stairs were in position. The door was open. All that was needed was for the PM to appear.

'What's keeping you, Jim?' The President's stage whisper was audible and brought smiles to the waiting party.

Suddenly there they were, Sir James and Lady Babbington. The PM was a tall Macmillan-like figure and his wife rather small and dainty. An unceremonious wave preceded their descending the steps.

Sarah had met the PM a number of times and had found him a courteous man with a ready sense of humour, something that endeared him to the public.

'Sarah, are you with us, or them?' he quipped, glancing sideways at the President, who was beside him.

'Depends on the rate of exchange, Sir!'

There was a gust of laughter as he moved on to greet the Ambassador.

Formalities were at a minimum, as were photographs: security saw to that.

'We'll do the public thing at the Cottage,' Duncan said easily. 'Let's board the chopper, and get outta here!'

*

Two lecterns had been set out for the leaders in the open air, and after freshening up they stepped out to meet the assembled media.

First the President welcomed a valued personal friend and also a true friend of the United States. He stressed their cooperation on the hostage crisis and their daily phone calls on the matter as well as other trouble spots.

The Prime Minister was equally brief, joking that he felt so much at home within the White House that he felt the next stage in his training would be washing up!

The press corps liked the quip and there was general laughter, at which time Duncan felt it right to ask for questions. The President picked Jeff Hoop, generally known as the resident awkward man. His questions were mostly provocative, yet often stimulating. Duncan liked him.

'Mr President, aren't we overplaying this special relationship thing?'

'Jeff, if I didn't mention it Sir James would think he'd landed in another country! Seriously though, I'm happy that we acknowledge our long-standing friendship, but I would be happier if such a relationship were extended to a wider circle. We all share a common humanity; we have common aspirations, yet how often we focus on the differences, instead of celebrating the amazing diversity of our one humanity. Prime Minister,' he added, turning to Sir James.

'Mr President, we used to think that God was English, but now the question's open for discussion.'

The President burst out laughing.

'Alas, we humans are a stubborn lot,' the PM continued, when the humour had subsided. 'We love our differences and much too often hate the differences we see in others.'

'Wise words, Prime Minister,' the President responded.

'Mr President,' a forceful questioner cut in. 'The US and Britain have two of the most sophisticated intelligence services in the world. Why are we so clueless? Why don't we know what happened to our people, for they went missing in a friendly country?' The sound of outrage was obvious.

'Frank,' the President responded, 'I have the same frustrations, but our friends are doing all they can. Tribal loyalties and fiercely held beliefs build walls of silence. We must be patient.'

'Zap the goddam walls,' a voice reacted.

'I wish it were so easy,' Duncan returned, sensing the build-up of emotion in the media ranks before him. 'I will repeat, patience is essential, for impulsive action will do more harm than good,' he concluded, turning bodily to Sir James.

'The unforgiving labyrinths that breed extremists are difficult to penetrate. We must not jeopardize the efforts of brave men,' the PM supported forcefully.

The President nodded while selecting the next questioner.

'Mr President, you have given us three questions related to location value. Are you questioning our property-owning tradition, and if so, does your British friend agree?'

'Alf, you haven't lost your touch, and rest content, your house is safe enough for it's your property. My questions are not directed at buildings. They focus on location value and Alf, I would like to leave my questions open, as answers quickly given end up on dusty shelves with equal speed.'

'But Mr President, my house is in a pleasant area. If it were somewhere else it could be half the price!'

'Yes, Alf, you've got it, but let's leave the three questions open, OK. Prime Minister, I must apologize for this domestic interlude. However, if you would like to say something, please do so,' Duncan smiled knowingly.

'It would not be appropriate for me to comment on US domestic issues. However, the questions, that is, what is location value etc., are plain and simple and could apply to any country, the UK included. The general comment I would make is this: reason should not be ignored. If I were to say more, you guys would be onto me for meddling!'

The questioning now switched to hopes of peace in the troubled areas of the Middle East. Both leaders were well briefed and spoke at length on the hopes and difficulties, and how they planned to discuss the matter in detail at Camp David. Indeed, in the wider sense, a joint approach to current problems was their aim.

The final question centred on multi-national corporations and the ethics of their business practices. This generated considerable heat from the radical elements that were demanding sudden and dramatic change. Both leaders counselled gradual reform, but this was grudgingly received.

'Reforming rules and regulations have their place but it's a change of heart that's needed. The Prime Minister and I fully agree on this. It's our attitude that needs to change. It's not unlike the environment, where a reverence for nature would transform our habits. So, in the workplace we need to respect our common humanity. Prime Minister?' the President added, inviting a response.

'I wholly agree with the President. We are all God's children. This simple memory can work miracles.'

'Well, folks, that's it. Thank you for your questions. And, folks, let's all pray the hostages will soon regain their freedom.'

After a brief wave, both men turned and walked briskly into the White House.

*

Inside, Sarah had been watching on the screen. Impressive, she thought, for the general lack of platitude. Perhaps a touch evangelistic at the end, but was that simply journalistic colouring on her part?

Chapter Eighteen

John Duncan felt that he was flying somewhere between faith and irresponsibility. One event followed another; indeed, they seemed to appear rather than follow. Outwardly nothing had changed, yet in some way everything had changed. Irreconcilable events would suddenly resolve, but right on the wire. It was almost uncanny and it alerted him to watch and listen and to act upon the promptings that arose.

One such prompting had been the promotion of Harry Roberts. It had simply happened and it had proved to be exactly right. Duncan still reflected on affairs, and many, if not the majority, of his decisions were accomplished in this way. But with the difficult decisions, when his advisors were divided he simply waited, until, conveyed by some strange sense of certainty, the answer came.

Sarah Crawford was a gift from God, but how and when to act was pending. Joss was full of fears about a girlfriend in the White House while a hostage crisis filled the headlines. He had a point, for in the President the people saw the symbol of the state. How he acted in a crisis would reap their instant praise or anger. So when it came to Sarah the President waited, as with his usual mode of thinking he had no idea what to do.

She would be present at Camp David for the next three days with her BBC hat on. So there would be opportunities to meet, but the other press folk would be there and watching every move. The whole thing was so childish.

After an enjoyable supper in the company of Jim and Catherine Babbington with Joss and Joan Johnson as the only guests, the President retired, feeling pleasantly tired. He awoke, though, feeling strangely ill at ease. While dressing, the mood persisted: there seemed to be no reason for it. Then Joss arrived with the papers.

'Paper boy as well! Vaunting ambition, Joss!' Duncan joked,

trying to forget his agitation.

'The press have gone completely mad. Listen to this one. "Kremlin White House and the Five Year Plan." Then it lists the stages of the take-over; couched in humour, but telling. This guy knows his stuff.'

'What stuff, Joss?'

'What you and Harry talk about.'

'Joss, you're a good man. Harry is a good man. I don't want any nonsense, OK. We're a team and you're my chief of staff, period.'

'Mr President, there *is* no problem. You're reading something that's not there!'

'Sorry, Joss, I'm ill at ease this morning. I've tried to shake it off, but it persists. Something's brewing and it's not an Irish stew!'

'Well, your questions on location value have disturbed a lot of people. It could lose us the election!'

'Perhaps I've raced too quickly for the line?'

'You've only asked questions. We could let the matter rest until after the election.'

'Joss, that's not my style.'

'Yeah, I guess it's not. You've never danced on the surface. You've always gone for it!'

'For what, Joss?'

'The truth, John – sorry the "John" slipped out.'

'Thank God for that.'

'Yes, Mr President!'

Both men laughed.

'Dammit, it's back again!'

'What, Sir?'

'The agitation; it's like foreboding. Something's wrong, Joss, but I've no idea what it is.' Duncan shook his head, indicating his incomprehension. 'Let's go downstairs to the office.'

Downstairs they were met by the press secretary, Billy Benson.

'The gang are howling like a pack of wolves. There's no rhyme or reason. You're "The Enemy of Enterprise", and the "Enemy of Stability". The *Post* is OK with "Leaders stand firm", and there are others of a similar nature but some have gone way off the screen!'

'It's an election year, Billy. Someone's stirring the pot!' Joss interjected.

'It's not Whitehead; he hasn't said a word!'

'He wouldn't; it would be Vince who'd stir it!' Joss returned.

They were standing in the corridor and, catching a glimpse of Harry in the distance, the President waved. They waited a few moments for the big man to arrive.

'Mr President, you waved.'

'Yes, Harry, have you read the papers this morning?'

'I have. They're fairly lively, Sir.'

'What's behind it, Harry?'

'I can only speculate, but I'd put the vested interests high up on the suspect list. They're the ones who know about location value – for real!'

'You mean the real estate moguls.'

'Yes, Sir.'

The President, recalling his conversation with Sam Whitehead, nodded pensively. Then he noticed Benson getting restless.

'Billy, you'd better go and face the mob, but if it gets too hot at the briefing, call me.'

'Well, that's it. But I still feel restless!'

'Mr President, there is one thing,' Harry began quietly. 'And I feel both you and Mr Johnson ought to know.'

'Hey, let's retreat to the Oval Office,' Duncan suggested, sensing something confidential.

Harry was the last one through and as usual the door closed noiselessly.

'When was the last time your security cover was checked?'

'Quis custodiet ipsos custodes?'

'Who will guard the guardians? Yes, Sir, and it's my reason for speaking. Two of your security guys I know from my Gulf days, and in my book they're criminals. It's the first time I've noticed them.'

'Yeah, they only joined the group last week,' Joss said. 'They are highly recommended. Harry, these guys go through the mincer!'

'I would transfer them, Mr Johnson,' Harry said fiercely.

'Jeez, Harry, I've never seen you quite so forceful,' Duncan interjected.

'Sir, this is the White House. The security detail should be beyond suspicion. Who screened these fellas? Who waved them through? Mr President, we should not be having this conversation.'

'Joss,' the President prompted.

'We must act immediately,' Joss responded. 'It could be an oversight built on an oversight and so on. I hope so. If not, we have a serious security problem, for someone in authority must have blinked on purpose. Meanwhile I'll have these two desert veterans checked out by someone who isn't in the loop.'

Johnson quickly left, leaving Harry and the President alone.

'Joss will deliver. He's like that!'

They had been standing, and the President suddenly took a seat. Harry followed his example.

'I woke up restless and ill at ease this morning. I have no idea why, but the agitation persisted, like a kind of foreboding. Now it's gone, just as mysteriously as it came. Somehow I don't think it's unconnected to what's been happening in the press or what you've just told us.'

'I can only tell you what I've read in a book or what I've half experienced. When you think of it, creation is a unity. Everything is contained in space and there's only one space, or at least that's the way I see it. So what am I saying? I'm saying that we live in a unified environment where tensions and agitations are picked up, especially by the sensitive. Of course, being connected to this wider unity more particular feelings may be observed. Who knows what you may have sensed this morning? But, Sir, you would need a wise man to help you with these questions.'

'Harry, you're doing just fine. Jeez, it's a quarter to nine. I'd better go and pay my respects to the PM and his lady. Hey, why don't you come with me and I'll introduce you.'

Duncan had acted on another impulse and it felt exactly right.

Chapter Nineteen

Seb Sebbson and Jake Crystal were enjoying their customary weekly luncheon in the Hay Adams Hotel on the corner of Lafayette Square. As usual Seb was complaining about the heat while Jake looked on quite cool and unaffected.

'Jake, you eat like a goddam bird,' Seb grumbled.

Seb must have told him that a hundred times, but Jake as usual made no comment.

'Seb, what goes with Duncan? He asks three questions then hangs them out to dry and doesn't say another word.'

'He doesn't need to, for all the anti-guys are making such a goddam fuss. Show me the guy who hasn't heard the term "location value".'

'We have some very bright young men who've majored in economics and business studies and they pour scorn on Duncan's location value questions. They don't get angry with me, of course, but they do with others who take the Duncan line.'

'What do you expect, Jake? These fellas have spent years studying. They don't want some guy telling them they've got it wrong, even if he is the President.'

'That explains the passion of the chat show experts!'

'Self-opinionated bores!' Seb reacted.

Jake smiled thinly. Seb had often fitted the description.

'They're not all bores! Some of them are very well informed.'

'Yeah,' Seb reacted sceptically.

'Goddammit, it's just hit me, you're with Duncan. I never thought I'd live to see it. Mind you, I admire the guy as well. Why don't we walk across the square and knock!' Jake knew the wine had freed him up and made him almost reckless, but he didn't care.

'I can't walk, Jake, every goddam step's a pain!'

'You eat too much!' Jake had never dared to say a thing like that before.

'Jake, it's one of life's fast dwindling pleasures,'

'TO Trading keeps you amused.'

'Those guys can't wait to kick me off my perch and, do you know something, I don't give a damn! And what have I achieved with all those endless office hours? - A fortune for myself! Big deal, I never thought of others and in the desert of old age why should they think of me? At least, Duncan's doing something. These three questions are not about amassing a fortune or getting re-elected; indeed, it could destroy his prospects. Jake, he's doing it because he knows it's right. That's why I admire the man.'

'Here, let me freshen up your glass,' Jake reacted, amazed at what was little more than a confession. 'Listen, I've got Joss Johnson's mobile number. We could buzz him and fix a meeting.'

'Jake, they're at Camp David with the Brits.'

'I'd forgotten.

They sat in silence briefly.

'Hey, Joe Smolensky was on the phone this morning,' Jake related, expecting a less than positive reaction.

'What was he after?'

'He was trying to unload a publishing house he doesn't want.'

'What about the site?'

'He's keeping that.'

'Surprise, surprise! You turned him down, I hope.'

'You bet. You have to read the small print with that guy!'

'You sure do!' Seb growled. 'I was bad enough, but Joe has the cold-blooded ruthlessness of an alligator!'

Jake said no more. The wine had helped both of them to loosen up and talk, but there was a measure to things and Jake decided not to push it further.

Camp David was sixty miles to the north-west of Washington in the Catoctin Mountain Park. Sarah hadn't been before and was full of anticipation. The trees would be magnificent, even though it was too late for the full glory of the Fall. She had expected to go by helicopter but was surprised to learn almost at the last moment that they were going by road. She was travelling with part of the British contingent: the Foreign Office officials who were the PM's advisors. The PM, of course, was travelling with the President.

Sarah and Joan Johnson had been driven to the White House but Joss had left much earlier and the night before he'd been continually on the phone. Sarah's journalistic instincts were alerted but she asked no questions and Joan, as ever, made no comment on her husband's activities, other than grumbling that he worked too hard. At the White House Sarah only had a brief glimpse of the President, before he disappeared into the limo, but he had smiled and waved. At least that was something!

Joss had persuaded the President to travel by road simply as a precaution. A routine schedule was best avoided. He had made enquiries via personal friends he had at Langley and was careful not to arouse any official curiosity. Again he had spoken to an old friend at the Pentagon who was the soul of discretion. If there were a rogue official in the pack, they needed to find him not scare him. In the meantime, the two security men had been given an 'important' assignment.

They arrived at Camp David in time for a late lunch, after which the President and the PM went for a walk without their officials. This didn't please the officials. Both men were aware of that but as neither took advantage of the other's lapses and asides, they found the freedom of a free exchange invaluable.

'Are our Gulf friends dragging their feet?' the PM asked. 'They're always so bloody polite it's difficult to know what they're thinking!'

'Yeah, I often feel we've no idea how they operate. Their tribal and family loyalties are a maze that only they can comprehend. For instance, we have men on the ground, but who in fact commands their loyalty when the chips are down? Mind you, there are some very brave men and we owe them a lot.'

'John, once they trust you, these bods are fiercely loyal and it's a bloody shame when we let such people down. That impressive man you introduced me to, Harry Roberts, he was over there.'

'Marine sergeant. Led an elite group, I believe.'

'What's *he* say?'

'He takes the softly-softly line.'

'A line I would expect. That guy's got his head screwed on.'

'He drove the Presidential limo, that's how I got to know him, and he was the only one who seemed to understand what I'd experienced on the morning of my so-called disappearance.'

'What did happen that morning, John?'

'Jim, it seems a long way distant now. At the time I woke up with a real downer, a Churchillian "black dog." Then something amazing happened. It was as if someone had turned up the lights at a TV interview. But it wasn't just an outer light; it was an inner light as well. Come to think of it, I wasn't aware of an inner and an outer. Everything was delightful, everything was interesting, and it lasted, though almost right away it began to fade.'

'So what did Harry say?'

'That he had a similar experience in the Gulf. He called it an expansion, a shot of higher awareness. Seeing 'face to face,' to borrow the well-known passage.'

'According to the books I've read, you've had a glimpse of reality.'

'Yes, Jim, we're usually "Sicklied o'er with the pale cast of thought."'

'The King James and Shakespeare and all in one morning – we're waxing lyrical, John.'

'Jeez, what would CNN not pay to have a disc of this?'

*

Chapter Twenty

The questions of sustainable growth and care for the environment were well-aired topics. Study groups attended by expert advisors to both the leaders discussed these topics exhaustively. There was no rivalry or friction between the two delegations, but progress was slow and difficult. To change one thing caused complications, often from a wholly unexpected quarter. It was a one-step-forward-two-steps-back situation where a positive communiqué promised to be little more than window dressing. Harry had observed throughout, but the complicated in-house talk was difficult to follow. There was little ground to stand on, as it were, and what there was kept shifting.

As far as he could see, the firm or business enterprise had two basic economic rules. That was to maximize profit and minimize costs. This seemed straightforward enough, but when human labour was viewed as a cost rather than the engine of production labour relations became an area of conflict. Of course, cheap imports could, and did, demolish profits overnight, and firms, seeking third-world labour costs, relocated. Redundancies, with their resultant hardships, followed, while accusations of 'slave labour' conditions attached to the third-world relocation sites. Again, the high level of tax levied on the home enterprise and the deadening weight of regulations made relocation inevitable in a free trade climate.

Harry stifled a yawn. This was hard work, even though it was the morning. Harry had been hoping for a break but there was no let-up. The debate ground on.

They talked of global giants with their mass production lines locked in competition and squeezing profit margins. Costs were slashed ruthlessly. Of course, high volume production and growth cut unit costs. So, coupled with the new industrial giants of the East, demand for raw materials was climbing steeply. For growth was the universal byword of success, but was it sustainable, and if not, how could it be modified, or humanized, as Harry thought. Somehow the human element had been forgotten. As the President kept saying, there *was* a moral imperative. The leaven of humanity *was* needed on a global scale, but how?

The mass of complication taxed Harry's power of attention to the limit. He could only admire the expertise displayed, but what was at the root of it all? He had been humbled by the scale of the difficulties, yet he knew that in ignoring natural economic law many of the problems were inevitable. Harry had no love for Marxist theory, but Karl had said one fundamental fact with clarity: that the expropriation of the people from the soil was the basis of the capitalist mode of production. Anyway, it was something like that. Harry didn't like the word 'capitalist' for, as far as he was concerned, Marx had been diverted by the word, which, for Harry, was a kind of smokescreen. But the expropriation of the people from the land had provided the fodder for the mass production factories and, although camouflaged, it was still doing it!

Harry felt it inappropriate to speak; indeed, to push his theories on these people would be clearly out of place. In any case, the discussion was drawing to a close and after the chairman's concluding remarks his mind was drawn to a brisk walk in the grounds. This didn't happen, for just as he made to leave the hall the Chairman, Freddie Wilkins, beckoned him.

'Mr Roberts, we have a free hour before lunch and I was wondering if you would like to join me for a walk.'

'That would be a pleasure, Dr Wilkins.'

'Freddie to you, Sir!'

'Only if you call me Harry.'

'It's a deal!' Wilkins smiled widely. He was a slim academic-looking man with spectacles and noted for the mildness of his manner.

'What a lovely morning and the weather forecast is good, I believe, so I'm thinking of staying for few days in Washington after the Summit. I've been a number of times to DC but it's always been an in and out, if you get my meaning.'

'Have you got somewhere to stay?' Harry asked politely.

'The Cosmos Club.'

'You'll like that, Freddie. It's quite near your embassy.'

'So I believe.'

The pleasantries continued for some time and Harry wondered when Freddie would get down to business. Obviously he hadn't suggested a walk for nothing. The Brits, of course, were not given to unseemly haste, so Harry waited.

'Harry, I was wondering what you felt about this morning's meeting?' The moment had arrived, Harry thought wryly.

'I was impressed with your grasp of the complicated data. I'm afraid you lost me frequently. Given the difficulty of changing anything or applying regulations, it seemed to me that a direct appeal to our better parts, that is our humanity, could be more effective than we think.'

'Interesting, Harry, please continue.'

'If a moral approach became "the done thing", as, I believe, you say in your country, perhaps standards would rise. All this may be wishful thinking but a change of attitude is a powerful thing.'

'I agree we need heart as well as head. It would be nice, though, if we had something substantial for the communiqué.'

'I sense an understatement, Freddie!' Harry smiled. 'I had some English friends in the Gulf!'

Freddie Wilkins laughed.

'Well, have you a lifeline? Is there something you can add?'

'I doubt if patching up the cracks will help; people aren't fooled by that. Somehow we need some shift at the root, in fact, where the causes are. These sweat shop factories we hear about. Why is there such a press of unemployed fighting for work, and poorly paid work at that? Why can't they get a patch of land and set up on their own?'

'They can't afford the rent or the money lender's interest.'

'You've got it, Freddie,'

'But, Harry, that's a can of worms!'

'Open the tin, and the worms will each find their own piece of earth. And, Freddie, they'll not take more than they need.'

'My God, I see where you're coming from! The big boys won't like that!'

'Tell them they need to give a little. We're not asking for it all, just a little!'

'How, Harry, how?'

'The President is keen on Latin aphorisms. *Laudando praecipere* is a favourite.'

'I know it – teach by praising. You're a clever old stick, Harry!'

Harry laughed.

'Old stick,' he repeated. 'I take it that's a compliment!'

'It's in that direction!'

Harry's laughter bubbled again.

'Look, there's the President walking with Sarah Crawford,' Wilkins pointed out. 'She's carrying a note pad, I see.'

Good ploy, Mr President, but Harry didn't say a word.

*

Chapter Twenty-One

The charade of giving a private interview lasted for five minutes. Duncan couldn't abide the pretence and said so openly.

'Sarah, I'm much too fond of you to continue with this pantomime. The truth is I can't keep my eyes off you and all I want to do is take you in my arms. But John Duncan is President of the United States and is constrained. He must not have a girlfriend in the White House during a hostage crisis, for he is, whether he likes it or not, the symbol of the state. Will you consider waiting for me, Sarah? And call me John; that is a Presidential Order !'

'Mr President, John, I'm a whirlpool of emotion. Joy has been released yet held in check, for I cannot throw my arms about you as I wish so much to do. We must keep walking and I must keep clutching at this notepad, for, John, the camera always wins.'

'Sarah, you're keeping me hanging out there! Will you wait?'

'Don't be silly, John, of course I'll wait!'

Duncan laughed.

'God, I feel normal. Imagine being called John and silly on the same day. What luxury!'

This time Sarah laughed and Duncan just managed to control himself. The sound was captivating. And the surrounding colours of the Fall lent their magic.

When it came, the joint communiqué reflected almost exactly the thinking of Freddie Wilkins and Harry Roberts. This was not surprising, as a common intention united the leaders and their advisors. All sensed that little could be achieved in the hard-nosed commercial side but that an appeal to humanity, if continually pressed, might persuade even the ruthless that it was in their best interests to modify their practice. Notwithstanding, questions could be asked. Why was there a mass of poverty-stricken jobless fighting for employment? Not only was it a question that the third-world leaders needed to address, it was a question for developed nations too: a tour of city slums soon made it clear that all was far from well. Why were the very rich so rich and the very poor so poor when the elements of air, water, sunshine and land were given to all?

The President and the PM took turns to articulate their message and, as ever with Sir James, humour was never far away. In conclusion, the British premier again emphasized their joint commitment to the hostages, before turning to the President.

Duncan followed this with an equally forceful statement. Then he paused, deliberately taking time to scan the assembled press, including them, as it were, one by one. Then he began to speak.

'With such abundance all around, clearly the good Lord intended no deprivation. It's we who've built our prison walls and we can tear them down. The wasteful luxury of the super-rich and deprivation of the poor cry out for remedy, not at the hands of a Stalin-like dictator, but at the cry of humanity that is in the heart of every human. It's time we stopped passing by on the other side.'

Sarah, who'd been amongst the Press, was emotional. This wasn't just rhetoric. John had meant it, every word! She watched him as he joked with Sir James. John's hair was quite grey, she observed wistfully. It suited him. She smiled to herself. Sarah, dear, you're gone, completely gone.

Two helicopters transported the principals to Dulles International, where the PM's plane was waiting. There was no official send-off, just a parting of good friends; another set piece would have gilded the lily. The British Ambassador, his wife, and Sarah along with Joss and Joan Johnson accompanied the President back to the White House. Harry Roberts with his new friend Dr Freddie Wilkins journeyed in the second helicopter together with others of the White House staff. The limos had been ready at Camp David, but Joss, using the same tactic as before, switched at the last moment to the choppers. He was still awaiting the report into the apparent breach in security.

With the President's connivance it had been agreed that Sarah should move to the Ambassador's residence. The Johnsons were content the way things were. But Duncan was concerned with security. Even though Sarah and he were observing a self-imposed quarantine, the bad boys, as Sir James would call them, could well see a kidnap opportunity. They weren't fools.

*

In the morning the Press were divided. 'Camp David Platitudes' was balanced by 'Good Samaritan speech rings true.' On the hostage issue the sober headline 'President pledges maximum intelligence effort' competed with 'Stop being Mr Nice Guy, get them back.' In the main the business commentators were cynical in tone. But one respected columnist argued that the President was right. 'Profit before people or people before profit, reflected the old tired confrontation of the past. What was needed was profit for all. This was practical morality.'

'I like it,' Harry muttered to himself. He lifted the phone but put it down again when the President appeared at the door.

'Have you read Ed Morrison?' Duncan asked

'Yes, Sir, he's on our wavelength.'

'He sure is.'

There was a knock and Joss suddenly was upon them.

'Hey, press the remote, CNN. I hope we haven't missed it!'

'There it is!' Joss said excitedly. 'The great Seb Sebbson has resigned from TO Trading. Who would ever have believed it? The Wall Street guys are buzzing like flies, but Seb doesn't seem to give a damn.'

'Time turns up surprises when we least expect them,' the President mumbled. 'What's Seb's angle? That guy always has an angle!'

'Maybe he's tired, Sir,' Harry ventured. 'These tycoons can implode. Suddenly all their work is nothing but a bloodless shell.'

'Well, well. No doubt we'll read about it tomorrow, in full. And I mean full! Have they named a successor?' Duncan asked, turning to his Chief of Staff.

'There hasn't been time. Apparently no one knew or suspected Seb was throwing in the towel!'

'Wall Street will be in mourning,' Duncan quipped.

'Only for a day, Sir,' Joss returned. 'A new tycoon is on his way!'

'And so it is with Presidents!' Duncan said quietly.

Chapter Twenty-Two

There had been intimations passed to intelligence that the hostages were alive, and, because of that, hope also was alive. But there were also fears bred from the lack of contact and the usual video. Who were the kidnappers and what was their aim? These questions had been asked a thousand times, or so it seemed, on prime time broadcasts. Frustrations were mounting, as were calls for action. At the same time John Duncan's commanding lead was being steadily eroded.

Three days after the Summit at Camp David intelligence was received that the hostages were alive and well. The tenuous information was confirmed by a code word only known to the office of the fact-finding mission, which had obviously been inserted by one of the hostages. This greatly boosted hope but, perversely, also boosted the strident cries for action from an 'inactive' President. So the ratings continued to slide.

Experts were greatly puzzled by the behaviour of the captors, for the usual publicity-conscious pattern was completely absent. There was so little to go on, no leads to follow, and the wall of silence was indeed a wall. This, however, did not stop the allegations of CIA ineptitude that were growing frequent. A powerful nation was demanding results.

Jake was worried, for his friend's sudden resignation had been without warning. A brief statement at TO's weekly meeting left the board in disarray and the Deputy Chairman making hurried statements to the press. And that was that. Seb Sebbson, President and CEO of TO Trading, had simply walked out. 'He was old, tired and he'd had enough. It was time for a new broom.' Such was the brevity of his parting words.

Jake, of course, had not been completely surprised, for his old friend had been acting oddly for some time. One thing had not changed: their luncheon date at their usual hotel on the corner of

Lafayette Square.

Seb looked younger when he entered the lobby and he seemed lighter on his feet.

'Jake!' he boomed. 'I'm a free man; I should have done this goddam thing ten years ago! Let's have lunch,' he added striding towards the restaurant.

Jake followed, finding Seb's transformation difficult to believe.

Once seated at their usual table, Seb launched into a description of his post-resignation world.

'No Dow Jones, no takeovers, no lawyers, no accountants! Jake, it's paradise. You know, I started in my father's general store and there I met the customers face to face. Those were happy times, for I was meeting people and never gave much thought to what we call the bottom line. Then father took over a company with two sites and so the game began. After that it was management and little else but bottom line.'

'Profit margins keep the show on the road!'

'Yeah,' Seb responded absently. 'Well, that's all past; now I've joined the living – and so should you! Why don't you retire?'

'I like my job.'

'Jake, you're bottom line, the same as I was. You hardly ever see your editors, except to fire them. And as for authors – well, you might see the odd celeb – good PR for the group, but that's the measure of it.'

'There's more to it than that!'

'Yeah, but not much – you're a slave to your Dow Jones listing! Hey, eat up, you're a goddam skeleton.'

'So what are you going to do with all your free time?'

'Free time! I haven't any. I'm twenty-four seven, for crissake!'

'Doing what?'

'I'm following everything Duncan says on this location thing and also on morality. That's a full time job, for he's the President and he's always talking.'

'But, Seb, it's mostly repeating what he said before.'

'You'd be surprised, there's always something new. And then there are the columnists. This morning, for instance, I just sent off an e-mail to Ed Morrison. Good article, I thought.'

'You're hooked, Seb; Duncan's got you on a line!'

'Jake, he's saying some good things.'

'Yeah, but he's only got a year. The way the polls are heading he'll never make a second term.'

'Goddam shame!'

'You wouldn't have said that a year ago!'

'I guess not. Maybe I oughta throw that guy a line.'

'How?'

'By writing to the press, and soon, before they forget who I am!'

'Seb Sebbson forgotten?! Never!'

'Good title for my autobi!' Seb threw back his head and laughed.

*

The President was in his private office when Joss knocked briefly and walked in.

'You've got a new ally, Mr President.'

'Who? I thought they were all going out the other end!'

'Seb Sebbson...'

'Jeez, you must be joking!'

'I'm not, there he is in black and white!' Joss handed the paper across and waited until Duncan scanned the content.

'Good letter, he knows his stuff.'

'And he's been following your speeches. He refers to three separate venues!'

'Yeah, and it's good hard-headed copy! Let's bring him in. There's that guy Pucci from New York and there's Ed Morrison and Seb. Yeah, let's have them all in. Let's encourage these folk. But Seb, who would have ever guessed? Harry always maintains that when people see the truth of this location message, the world lights up, but you can't say that too loudly, Harry cautions, as the folk are quick to think you're nuts. "You mean to say you know," they say, "and all the others don't? Yeah, yeah, big deal!" they grunt, and turn away! That's how Harry put it and it sounds exactly right.'

Chapter Twenty-Three

Ed Vince was bubbling with enthusiasm. Everything was going well. Already the Senator was level-pegging with the President and the President's trend was down and liable to continue. All they had to do was keep the ship on course. Funds were simply flowing in. Nothing could stop them. Sam Whitehead would be president. The Senator's cousin, recruited as a strategy guru, was much more cautious. A year was a long time and politics a fickle game.

Sam Whitehead himself had few illusions. Leading the polls was the gift of the hostage crisis and it would be crass, and plainly stupid, to play that card and join the populist clamour. Ed would have done it, the Senator guessed. Thank the Lord he'd chosen cousin Hal, for he had stamped on that immediately.

They were still receiving overtures from Smolensky, keen to be associated with the winning team, but Hal had stamped on that as well. Hal was a good choice but Ed was a disaster, yet sacking him could cause unwanted friction. Ed was a likeable devil, but he needed someone stable at his side.

Even though it had been weeks ago and even though he had warned the President, the cold vindictive sound in Smolensky's voice still haunted him. That guy was bad news and he had the cash to make the bad news real. Seb Sebbson had been a turn-up, though. Who would have ever guessed that that would happen? Certainly not the GOP front-runner. Sam Whitehead smiled to himself. What a game it was. Seb was Duncan's man, but Whitehead didn't mind. In fact, he rather admired John Duncan, for he wasn't a populist. He wasn't playing to the gallery. If he were he'd have given location value a wide berth, for real estate was the bedrock of privilege and nowadays privilege was widely spread in the affluent, and aspiring, suburbs.

Initial investigations into the White House security lapse had revealed nothing. Because of this Harry was approached about possible mistaken identity but he remained absolutely positive about his accusations. The two men he had identified were not trustworthy and he suggested contacting the officer in the field at the time.

'He'll know, for these guys were notorious,' Harry said emphatically, 'but they always managed to avoid the can.'

The officer, a general now retired, confirmed all that Harry said and Joss, still intent on keeping the matter under wraps, commissioned him to make further 'private' enquiries. Joss, careful as ever of the political fall-out, was much more hopeful. Once he had documented facts he could act. For, confronted with hard evidence, the departments concerned could not wriggle and deny responsibility.

Another major concern, if not *the* major concern, was the hostage crisis, for it was relentlessly destroying the President's lead. It was election year and the kidnappers would surely know this all too well. So Joss feared that the crisis could drag on and on and there was nothing he could do about it, nothing at all.

Joss, of course, did not betray his concern either to the White House staff or publicly. He was much too good a pro for that, but he did confide in his friend the President.

'JFK's friend Macmillan put it in a nutshell – "Events, dear boy, events", or at least something like that. Joss, we can't beat City Hall. It's the way it is, but we can do our best while we're here. Tell me, did you ever get any feedback on alternative fuels?'

'The big corporations in the fuel and energy business all have R&D but it's not politically driven. It's commercially driven. That's the feeling I get. In other words, their survival doesn't immediately depend on it.'

'It proves the old saying that necessity is the mother of invention. It's a pity necessity has to hit us with a truckload of bricks before we act! Keep pushing, Joss. And, Joss, we're bringing in Seb, Leo Pucci and Ed Morrison. Harry probably told you.'

'He did.'

'He's chairing the meeting and I'll slip in somewhere in the middle.'

'That guy seems to cope with anything we throw at him. You know, he still calls me Mr Johnson.'

'Let it be, Joss, I like this old-world courtesy.'

'Yes, Mr President.'

'That's new-world, Joss!'

Both men laughed.

*

If the trend continued John was going to lose. It was a tragedy, especially for America. Sarah had entertained dreams of being First Lady; that was only natural, but it was secondary. John himself was the prize: easy-mannered John, carrying his unique ability almost casually. He was perceptive and his thinking rarely lingered on the surface. Doing what was right instead of what was popular appeared to be a characteristic of his policy. This, of course, gave Joss Johnson kittens, trying, as he was, to keep the ship of politics on even keel.

Joss, of course, was a life long-friend and Harry a new and rather special confidant. It was Harry who had understood John's walk-about and those heightened moments of awareness that had come to him. Harry, too, was an initiating influence on the question of location value. This was head to head against the vested interests. They would fight and her journalistic instinct knew the fight would be an all-out war, that was, unless the body of the people were persuaded that the issue held the key to urban peace. The tolerance of grinding poverty living side by side with wasteful luxury was surely not an option. 'Even she could see it', Sarah muttered to herself. The argument that the poor were lazy and incapable of effort spoke of blindness, if not arrogance. Such was the arrogance that drove the people directly into the waiting arms of militants.

She longed to talk about these things with John and the few words on their mobiles only made things worse. Sometimes in her weakness she blamed him for excessive scruple. It was a modern world and not a medieval one. Yet she knew she would not have it otherwise. In the meantime she would read, conduct some bland and unexciting interviews, and continue with her 'Letters from the Embassy' that the BBC were sending out on radio.

*

Chapter Twenty-Four

Leo Pucci was an Italian American and looked it, but his voice was uncoloured by such ancestry. He was a small man with a kind of punchy energy. In contrast Ed Morrison acted like a reticent Scotsman more at home in the study of a manse than amidst the glare of political journalism. As it was, Ed's ancestors had long left Scotland, and Ed, himself, had never visited the place. Seb didn't know his ancestry, for his father, who'd been born in New York, refused to talk about it, but most guessed that it was middle Europe.

Harry welcomed them all warmly, explaining the President's wish that they might meet on a fairly regular basis to discuss the issue of location value as spelled out by the President's three questions and perhaps more fundamentally the question of the natural law and the nature of society.

'The President hopes that these discussions will be subject to what his friend the British PM calls the Chatham House Rule. In other words we don't want to see our deliberations on a billboard in the morning.'

'Harry, that's all right by me. But hey, you speak in an English kind of way!'

'I had a number of close friends in the Gulf who were English, Mr Sebbson. I guess it must have rubbed off.'

'Hey, none of this mister stuff, it's Seb.'

'Mr Sebbson, your experience and age demand respect.'

'Jeez, nobody's ever said that to me. OK, Harry, play it your way.'

'The President hopes to join us shortly,' Harry continued, 'and he'll no doubt fill you in. But more than anything, he's interested in your views and how we can tackle reform and address the curse of poverty. Well, folks, that's the formal set-up. Over to you.'

'Harry, this location-value thing is self-evident. Even I can see it. Why is it being ignored?'

'Leo,' Seb growled, 'we're all too goddam selfish. We all want to be billionaires and too hell with the other fella.'

'I'm not so sure,' Ed Morrison cut in. 'I don't think it's as simple as that. I just think we can't see past the everyday reality. For most of us that reality is the furniture of our life. It's what we know! New ideas are mistrusted. It's like the office – the boss decides to change the layout and the place erupts.'

'Ed, people are not stupid,' Leo countered. 'We need some way to make them stop and think.'

'Well, I think that it's this moral angle that we need to work on,' Seb said forcefully. 'We need to touch the heart. That's why I changed, the President got to me. And if he got to me he can punch through any goddam wall!'

'You're just a softie, Seb!' Leo quipped, and there was an instant burst of laughter.

Just then the President arrived.

'You fellas seem to be enjoying yourselves!'

'Mr President,' they said in near unison. Seb struggled with the others to stand up.

'Be seated, gentlemen. It's real good to see you. You're all busy men and I appreciate you being here. So, Harry, what have you discovered?'

Harry quickly summarized the conversation.

'I like all your points. Every one is valid and, as Seb has emphasized, the moral angle is the sharp edge of our thrust. We need to shift the compass point, but slowly, as haste would cause disruption and injustice and, what is maybe worse, discredit the whole idea of what we are about. Now, I know I've just arrived, but I've been pressed to meet an Ambassador who wants to see me urgently. Anyway, I'll see you later in the Blue Room.' The President smiled. 'I believe refreshments are being served! So if you'll excuse me...'

'Mr President,' they all intoned.

'He's got a way with words,' Seb said in what sounded like a stage whisper. 'And this business of discrediting the whole idea: what is the whole idea? What are we about? You know, I was big on the Street, but this is big, I mean real big. I've just got a whiff of it. Move the compass slowly, yeah, but not too slowly. Jeez, I want to move it all the way!'

Harry laughed.

'You've got it, Mr Sebbson, for when you see the logic of it all you want to tell the world. The simplicity is so simple that most believe we're nuts. Earnings belong to the earner and location value in the midst of a community belongs to the community. That's the bare bones of the principle; then it's fleshed out and amended by the practical.'

'And that's where the trouble starts,' Leo Pucci interjected.

'The trouble is already there. The art is in the application of simplicity, and, Leo, that ain't simple!'

'And here's where we need the professionals,' Ed cut in.

'But ones who know the simple principle,' Harry cautioned. 'The waters can be muddied real easy.'

'Hey, you fellas are depressing me! I'm sticking to the moral angle; we need to touch the nation's heart. That block of tenements where most are unemployed or unemployable; you know, the one we pass in our air-conditioned limo and hardly notice – why do we tolerate such rat-holes, *why*, for crissake? OK, they get handouts, but handouts often make it worse. Those guys need hope, the chance to get up off their backsides! And you know something, we have the goddam key. Jeez, there is so much to do!'

Harry smiled. Seb was fired up.

'I know what you're thinking, Harry: move the compass slowly, but not too goddam slowly!'

Harry laughed.

'Well, gentlemen, this is our first meeting and we are the founder members of a group that may well grow to be a force for change. Now I think it's time for the Blue Room, where the conversation can continue and where the President will join us. There's one thing, though, I'd like to add. We all have talents. Ed and Leo are respected writers and you, Mr Sebbson, are persuasive on your feet; in other words, you can move an audience. You too have a way with words. The thing is, how can we use our various bents to further principles that now are dear to us? How can we serve our fellows? And gentlemen, move...'

'The compass slowly!' Seb completed. 'Goddammit, Harry, I think you *are* English. You've picked up that formal way of speaking. I like it!'

'Well, I did work closely with them in the desert.'

Special Forces, Seb mused knowingly. He would bet on it.

*

Chapter Twenty-Five

The conversation in the Blue Room was vigorous and continued for well over an hour. The President spent some time listening to their views, but reluctantly had to leave to see the Joint Chiefs.

'A review of the deterrent,' Duncan quipped. 'That's assuming that the other lot are sane enough to be deterred!'

It was close on six o'clock when the three men eventually took their leave. Harry, returning to his office, almost collided with the President as he emerged from the meeting with the Joint Chiefs.

'Was the day worthwhile, Harry?' Duncan probed.

As often was the case, Harry didn't answer immediately.

'It was, Sir. We got to know each other and we established common ground.'

'Harry, we can't push these people.'

'Mr President, the plain truth is, I've no idea what the next move is.'

'That's a relief!'

Harry laughed.

'Hey, we've both been at the coalface and it's after six, let's have a glass of something. My office cupboard has a few surprises!'

'Thank you, Sir.'

The President pointed to the office easy chair and the big man took his seat.

'What's it to be, Harry?'

'You had a nice red the last time, Sir.'

'Good choice. I'll join you.'

They savoured the wine in silence for some time.

'I was listening to the Joint Chiefs today, and as usual they were frightening me to death. Dear God, the scenarios they come up with! Anyway, I was dutifully listening when all at once there seemed to be another fella beside me – a familiar presence but a stranger just the same; a strange will-o'-the-wisp character. I even turned to see him, but he turned too! It was a kind of a rerun of the experience I had before.'

'We might even call this guy a shady character!' Harry responded.

They both laughed.

'Well, it looks as if I'm stuck with him,' the President returned. 'There certainly hasn't been another morning-in-the-park.'

'Those moments cannot be induced. I always feel they come when need commands.'

'Well put.'

'This is a really nice wine, Sir.'

'Yeah, the White House cellar is a real perk! Harry.'

'Yes, Sir.'

'I'm thinking of sending you to London for a day or two. I want you to meet the Brits who're working on the hostage situation. The PM knows. In fact, he welcomes it.'

'I thought that some of our fellas were already there.'

'They are but they'll be primed. You'll only be observing. I read your full CV yesterday. Joss gave it to me. Jeez, what haven't you done?'

'That's the trouble, Sir – the things I haven't done!'

Duncan laughed.

'Harry, just watch and listen. Nothing may happen; on the other hand, you may notice something. We're trying every which way!'

'I understand, Sir.'

'And Harry, if you want to state your views, see the PM.'

'When do I go, Sir?'

'As soon as you can, but tomorrow morning would be fine!'

Again there was laughter.

Harry flew from Andrews Air Force Base early in the morning, by US military transport, and arrived at Northolt by early evening and was met by his friend Dr Freddie Wilkins.

Both men chatted amiably as their Jaguar limo sped them down the A40 towards central London. Harry was surprised that two police outriders were escorting them. Clearly he'd been given the treatment but he made no comment.

'Where are you taking me, Freddie, Paddington Green?'

'The cells aren't big enough. No, my friend, I've managed to prevail upon a Pall Mall club to put you up. HMG thought it might be cheaper. The PM's on an austerity drive!'

Harry said nothing until they pulled up outside the dignified façade of the Reform Club. He knew exactly where he was, for he'd been before with a Brit friend from his Gulf days.

'Freddie, you've really hit the button. To me, this is tops. I have no love for overrated highly priced hotels.'

Dinner was leisurely and the conversation easy and relaxed. Freddie was good company. The location value issue was discussed in depth but not over-laboured. Freddie had more faith in pressure groups outside the political scene. Even so, a statesman in the right place and at the right time was a powerful force. Sir James was such a person, but his party, indeed all parties, had their eye on issues that were popular. Even so, Sir James was not a man to give up easily. Throughout most of Britain's modern history, he argued, the vested interests just gave way in time. Concessions lately given, yet still concessions, had saved the nation. This, he kept repeating, was again the duty of the hour. The rich were getting richer and the poor were sinking further. And this could not go on unheeded for too long.

They 'disappeared' into the easy chairs dotted generously in the lounge and when the clock swept round to half past ten Freddie took his leave.

'A memorable evening, Freddie: you've been a prince!'

'What, not a goddam prince, as Salinger kept repeating!' Freddie jested.

They parted warmly.

The next morning an MOD official arrived at 9am. Harry, of course, had been warned and was waiting in the lobby. He had also been warned that he would be having lunch at Number Ten. Harry had seen it all in the desert; he was not consumed with worry, but it concerned him that too much reliance was being put on his opinion. Well, he hadn't planned it. That's the way it was.

After being driven the short journey to Whitehall, Harry was whisked by a backstairs route to a basement theatre, where officials were setting up viewing equipment. Harry took a seat as indicated and waited.

A group of specialists was waiting and the presenter, armed with a pointer, began to describe the grainy images appearing on the screen. In Harry's case it was all very familiar.

'We are almost certain that we've located the site where the hostages are being held.' The speaker's voice was matter-of-fact. 'The latest intelligence, just received, is emphatic that no violence has taken place. In other words, the hostages are well in health. We calculate that special-forces can take this place with ease.'

'How many hostages would we lose in such an assault?' someone asked.

Harry grew agitated as the predictable discussion proceeded. The assumption of an armed attack, as being the only way, was common. Indeed, there was something very strange about the whole affair. The hostage-takers had not exploited the media weapon. They had not submitted any lurid video. Intelligence had reported no evidence of violence in the compound. Who were these people? Were they some altruistic sect pursuing some naïve scenario? And if they were benign, why were the hostages being held so long? Were they being subject to a brainwashing drug-related programme? Harry was completely foxed, but he knew one thing. Armed assault was most unwise until the facts were known. Difficult as it was, Harry held his tongue. Even in the coffee interval he kept his peace. Could it be that in a land of fierce tribal violence there had grown up a group of peaceniks, to use the almost vulgar western term?

At last Harry was released and escorted in the most deferential way to Number Ten. In fact, it was only a short walk.

Sir James Babbington was his usual witty self and his natural warmth was obvious. He enquired after his friend the President and Joss Johnson and then with pre-lunch drinks in their hands the questions started.

'Harry, I've a lot of time for your opinion and I know the President has as well. What did you think of this morning's briefing?'

'Prime Minister, I was bursting to ask questions, but the President instructed me to hold my peace until I spoke to you. Now I can speak.' Harry then listed all the facts and findings of the briefing and the questions that he felt were still unanswered. 'Sir', he continued, 'it would be madness to attack by force of modern arms when there is no evidence of violence. How our folk are being held we do not know. The overheads show nothing and intelligence cannot penetrate the wall of silence. Twice we have approached their so-called lair but, in the meantime, they had moved. They are behaving like nomads. Now we feel we have them cornered – so we think! But of one thing I feel certain. We must not kill when no one has been killing. Guns are guns, Prime Minister. You cannot call the bullets back.'

'Restraint is difficult to sell. The people cannot understand why we simply can't go in there!'

'And that's exactly how I'd feel if we'd received the usual video. But we haven't. When I was over there an English friend lent me a battered paperback of the *The Seven Pillars*.'

'T.E.Lawrence?'

Harry nodded.

'Lawrence writes about meeting "a grey-bearded, ragged man, with a face of great power and weariness" who came upon him while he was washing. According to Lawrence, the old man groaned: "The love is from God; and of God; and towards God." The passage had a powerful effect on me and made me think again when dealing with these people.'

'Are you saying that the desert has produced another holy man?'

'I'd be named a loony if I did. No, Sir, it makes me cautious. We've been approaching this from the usual hostage crisis mind-set. The fear of a blood bath has kept us at a distance, yet intelligence seems to indicate that such a fear is groundless. Nothing ties up and the usual conclusions don't fit. For instance, if there's been no coercion, why no mobile calls? Why no messages? Perhaps we're missing something very simple.'

'Harry, patience is a virtue that is running out. We can't sit on our hands for ever!'

Chapter Twenty-Six

After elaborate security precautions the boy was allowed into the British Embassy lobby. He was shy and his wide eyes scanned the opulence with wonder.

'I was told to give this letter to a senior official, Sir.' The boy said respectfully to the receptionist. 'It's very important,' he added. 'And I was told to wait for a reply.'

'Can I see that?' a distinguished-looking man called out as he approached.

Opening the letter carefully, the man began to read.

'Good God!' he exhaled.

Why are you still calling us hostages? The hand-written script began. *We are guests! Already five letters have been sent to reassure our people but we're told you keep repeating that we're being held. So we must assume the letters to have gone astray. This time we've sent our letter by a different hand and also to a different place, Amman. You may wonder why we haven't used our mobile phones. This is in deference to our Host, who feels the airways are polluted by such traffic – anyway the batteries are gone. Radios are also unpopular. Please remember that we are a fact-finding mission and that we're doing just that!*

'This changes everything,' the official whispered loudly. 'Bill, see that this young man is given refreshments and if he wants he can rest up for the night. Tomorrow we'll drive him to the border.

'You've come a long way,' he said gently to the boy.

'Yes, Sir.'

The news was flashed immediately to London and Washington; indeed Harry was lunching with the PM when the word arrived.

'You're thoughtful, Harry,' Sir James ventured.

'Losing five letters isn't just careless; it's deliberate!'

'For what reason?'

'What if someone wanted us to attack and were feeding us duff information? What if the bad guys were setting it up, in fact using us as their assassin? What if the Host, as our people call him, was the intended target?'

'The way you people think!' the PM exhaled.

*

Seb Sebbson had always been a popular after-dinner speaker. Now there was a difference. It wasn't just jokes and anecdotes. Now he had something to talk about, and instead of being reluctant to accept engagements he was willing to attend. Tonight it was a lawyers' dinner, the first engagement since he'd been converted, as it were, to Duncan's way of thinking.

'You fellas,' he began pugnaciously, 'are not lawyers, you're in the cock-up industry, the divorce industry, and the fighting-over-the-cake industry! And if we weren't so goddam stupid all of you would be redundant. But have no fear! We've all got doctorates on the subject. Then there are the no-win-no-fee guys. They're like monkeys on your shoulder. But, folks, that's nothing set against the real estate bonanza. Here, you fellas infiltrate the very steel of every tower block. But hey, you're only doing what we've asked you to. We can't shake hands, we can't agree without the lawyers' stamp and that can be a tidy sum. The sad fact is we cannot do without you, for guys like me have always had a team of lawyers round them. Otherwise we'd all have ended up on the chain gang, breaking rocks!'

Seb then had them rocking in their seats with colourful encounters from his early thrusting days. There seemed to be an endless stream of these. Theatrically he paused and took a drink.

'We have our differences, but the one thing that unites us all is tax. We all detest it and employ you fellas who help us to avoid it. In fact, without you guys the IRS would hang us out to dry.' Seb stopped, searching the ceiling of the restaurant with apparent interest. 'Seriously, though, why does the taxman wind us up? Somehow we feel outraged at all their prying. It's more than just the cash. We feel it's not their goddam business and that seems to be instinctive. Yet, taxes are necessary for the public need. So, are we simply being selfish or have we got a point? It seems natural to resent the plunder of our earnings. But what is natural when it comes to public needs? Has the city, state, community – call it what you will – has *it* got a natural fund that's being plundered? Look to Manhattan and ask yourself the question.

'Now, folks, I've overdone my after-dinner sound bite, and busy lawyers need some shuteye. But before we close I'll leave with the thought: If you want to halt the creeping plunder of your earnings, find the natural fund that runs the state!'

*

The next morning one paper managed to print the final part of Sebbson's speech at the Willard Hotel. They must have held the printing back, Joss thought, but there it was, the final punch line in bold type; *If you want to halt the creeping plunder of your earnings, find the natural fund that runs the state.* Above that in large print were the words; 'Sebbson lectures lawyers at the Willard.' Joss knew it would please the President but yet again, as Chief of Staff, Joss could only think it was a dangerous game to play in an election year.

The major story in the press was the welcome news from Amman, but contrary to expectation, outrage at the CIA ineptitude was general. What had they been doing these last months? Joss was worried as the fierce attacks were linked on more than one occasion with the 'Nice Guy' President. Indeed, a complacent White House was a common sentiment. This was not good copy and, in an election year, it could seed disaster.

The phone went on his special line. It was the President.

'Did you read Seb's speech? What a line! And in bold type too! I must phone him and clap him on the back. A memorable line – "If you want to halt the creeping plunder of your earnings find the natural fund that runs the state."'

'Seb's a natural. But, Sir, I don't like the sound of this 'hostage' thing. The complacent White House jibe, and the 'Nice Guy' President are not good copy in an election year!'

'They'll forget it over Christmas!'

'I hope so, Sir.'

'When's Harry back?'

'Tomorrow.'

'Good – Joss, don't bother to come up. I'll see you in the Oval Office in ten minutes.'

Chapter Twenty-Seven

With the hostage scare over, John Duncan felt himself now free of self-imposed restraint regarding Sarah. Joss Johnson had resigned himself to this, even though he feared a negative impact on the President's re-election prospects. Public sentiment was fickle and unpredictable and Sarah, being English, could be a downer. 'What's wrong with our American Girls?' could engender resentment. And when he thought of all the endless polls that could emerge, it made him cringe.

Joss knew too well that his friend John Duncan would be unmoved by such considerations, so he didn't even bring the matter up. Instead, he simply waited until the President might speak. That came sooner than he thought

Joss was waiting in the Oval Office when the President arrived.

'Sorry, Joss, I've kept you waiting, but I was on the line with Sarah. We were talking about Christmas and I suggested Camp David, which seemed to please her. What do you think, Joss?

'Will it be a large party, Sir?'

'No, just a few close friends - you and Joan, of course: Andy and his wife and Harry, yes Harry and Mary. There may be more, but the more I ask the more I need to ask. And Joss, in case you're worried, Sarah and I won't be mooning around. Our relationship needs to reflect a certain measure of dignity fitting this office. Jeez, that sounds pompous, but you no doubt get the drift. Well, with that off my chest, what's on the menu?'

'The Brazilian Ambassador at ten and the CIA director in the afternoon – Those are the two main callers. It's a fairly light schedule,' Joss responded.

'Yes, Joss, I've heard that one before.'

Harry returned mid-morning of the following day and reported in full to the President, Joss Johnson and the Secretary for Defence, Rod Rosewell.

Harry gave the general outline of his conversations with the PM's advisors. The Brits had been annoyed at the naivety of the fact-finders and had ordered them to report in regularly. Respect for their Host needed to be tempered with some common sense, they were told. Naturally the boy was shadowed; in fact, he was given transport for the greater part of the journey, so the Brits knew exactly where the party was located. Phone calls, made with the new mobiles handed to the boy, were almost immediate. So all was well.

'The sensibilities of the Host have not been too rudely violated, I hope?' the President interjected.

'Tact, the PM told me, was the keyword.'

'Is there anything else, Harry?'

'It's the missing messages that concern me. I don't mean the actual messages, as they were hardly strategic, no, it's why they went missing. Was it deliberate? We don't know and, again, too much fuss could cause more trouble than it's worth. Quite honestly, Sir, I would have these people back as soon as possible.'

'I agree!' Rod Rosewell interjected. He looked every bit a West Point man turned civvy. 'They've been out there long enough! It all sounds a bit Arab-loving- sentimental.'

'Harry,' the President prompted.

'Let's have them back. Let them report and then we can decide!'

'Let's do it!'

'Harry, how did the British press react?' Joss asked.

'They grumbled about the usual embarrassing ineptitude, but mostly concentrated on the fact that all were safe, but here I'm told the temperature has risen.'

'The CIA and a complacent White House are the targets.'

'Clever headlines come real easy. But creeping up on mud-bricked dwellings in the desert doesn't. I'd be the last to criticize the undercover fellas. The press should cool it.'

'Gentlemen, that's it.'

It had happened overnight as if someone had dropped a curtain. Suddenly a security detail was always in attendance. In the past she'd watched such things and wondered how the individuals felt. Now her learning curve was real. When she went to the centre the FBI was her transport. No matter where she went there was always protection. Strangely the press were quiet, perhaps because there'd been no public walking out. In fact, Camp David would be the first clear statement, as it were.

She needed Christmas presents and went shopping with Joan Johnson and although there was the usual security presence, the press were still quiescent. John, of course, had made no public statement and there'd been no questions from the briefings. Sarah guessed it was the lull before the storm.

Their friendship was a gentle, tender, loving thing. Histrionic demonstrations were not John Duncan's style. Sarah couldn't quite believe at times that it was actually happening. She was in love with the President of the United States and he in turn with her.

She was a frequent visitor to the White House, but John insisted that she leave before eleven. She liked the rather old-world attitude. It wasn't political caution, for his political incaution was forever giving Joss a headache. He was, of course, ever conscious of the function of the President. In his position, he kept saying, standards were important.

Sarah was British and in Britain the Queen was head of State. She could remain aloof from the daily free-for-all of politics and there were no elections to contend with. The President didn't have that luxury. Indeed, the role of President was far from easy, yet it worked and had been working from the time of George and Martha, as Americans were wont to call the first President and Lady.

Her ideal was a quiet marriage, but when the President was your future husband such dreams were idle. Like the President, she would be, in some ways, public property. So much was coursing through her mind. It was difficult to be calm, but in John's company it was easy. He was remarkably quiet in himself despite the burden that he carried. His conversation was rarely mundane and predictable. Only yesterday he'd told her how he'd suddenly connected with a reservoir of stillness, deep, cool, crystal in its clarity and what's more, he'd had the sense that it was always there. Memorable, he had added. 'Perhaps I'd stopped thinking for a while,' he joked. 'The pale cast of thought', she'd murmured, recalling her Shakespeare, and there the matter rested.

*

Chapter Twenty-Eight

'*Senator, Joe Smolensky's* giving a pre-Christmas party in Des Moines. We gotta go!' Ed Vince pressed his boss, the GOP front-runner.

'No way, Ed!' Sam Whitehead snapped. 'We don't need that guy!'

'A lot of big hitters are going. It won't look good if you're not there!'

'You go, Ed, but don't promise that fella anything, OK. Don't even stroke his goddam cat!'

'He doesn't like cats!'

'It's the cats that don't like him! And Ed, take Hal with you. I don't like it. Smolensky's trying to muscle in and he's throwing money at us. Remember, Ed, no deals!'

Why was the Senator so set against Smolensky, Vince wondered. OK, Joe had cut some corners in his time, but he wasn't the only one. Anyway, the Smolensky Corporation was big, real big. Only last week they'd swallowed up a large electrical group. But Joe still looked as he always had, a fight-scarred boxer. He dressed well and his suits were from the top shelf. Ed had always found him friendly and approachable; in fact, he liked him.

Joe Smolensky had fought for everything. Even when he was a boy he had fought. He'd had to, with an alcoholic mother and a father not much better, he'd been the one to scrape up money for the landlord's rent collector. Joe was always on the look-out, snapping up each opportunity as it came. He had one friend, an old half-crippled man who ran a corner shop three blocks away. Joe was his messenger and, grateful for Joe's diligence, he allowed the boy to display items he'd picked up in the trashcans of the rich. Joe was grateful and never cheated on the old boy and when he died Joe found that he'd inherited the shop. Joe Smolensky's career had begun.

Joe had trained himself to be ever watchful and alert, and apart from the old cripple few real favours came his way. Joe may have inherited the shop, but he had also inherited the rent and, as usual, the landlord never failed to call. Joe nicknamed him 'the shark' and he looked like one. Joe despised his grovelling manner but also noted that 'the shark' was receiving rent for virtually nothing in return. And Joe's little shop wasn't the only place 'the shark' was visiting. This was a dollar factory, Joe concluded, the easy way to bring it in. But how could he build up the cash he needed for the real estate? That bridge was very hard to cross. Then he had a windfall, an old-fashioned painting of a religious scene pushed into a trashcan, in the area where he still scavenged. He showed it to one of his corner-shop customers and noted that the man became excited but tried to hide the fact. Joe wouldn't sell but took it to a dealer, who in turn was equally excited. Again, he wouldn't sell and putting on his best suit he took it to the top dealer in New York, where the figure he received was well beyond his wildest dreams. At last, Joe was on the real estate ladder. Now *he* would collect the rent. And, again, he could forget the boxing game.

All this was casually going through his mind as he watched the guests swilling down his liquor. Free booze always pulled them in. Joe continued to watch as he had watched in the corner shop. In some strange way he saw them as the enemy, all wanting to steal something when he wasn't looking. Joe's backslapping friendly manner was an act, a way to engineer a deal or get to know some information. His was a lonely world that he packed with endless work and drinking parties with his aides. Somehow Joe could not join in. He was always apart, and because of that a lonely man. Although he would never admit it, Joe secretly envied the 'traitor' Sebbson, as he called him. Something that the bitterness of his stinging barbs betrayed.

'Have you read the latest braying from Duncan's donkey?' he called to Ed Vince as he passed.

'Meaning, Joe?'

'The great Seb Sebbson, the turncoat of the year!'

'Yeah, the scourge of the IRS!' Ed retorted grandly.

'That guy's out to lunch. Natural fund, what natural fund for crissake? Jeez, does he think there's manna from heaven?'

'Joe, I like it! News flash! Duncan's new budget proposals! Manna from Heaven!'

Smolensky laughed loudly, but as usual it was studied, as was the friendly slap on Ed Vince's back.

'Ed, that glass of yours is empty!'

'Joe, thanks for pointing out the oversight!'

'The Senator's not here, I see,' Joe said casually.

'He was going to try, I know,' Ed lied, 'but he's 24/7. He never stops.'

'The ratings are looking good. And Ed, you know, if there's anything I can do...'

'Yeah, thanks,' Ed reacted almost nervously, ever conscious of the Senator's warning. 'You're a real prince and what you're doing here is appreciated, much appreciated. Friends will not be forgotten.'

Hogwash, Joe thought cynically, while smiling in response. The door was still slammed shut and Whitehead would be present if he really wanted to.

'You know, Ed, if it wasn't for the Senator, I'd pitch in myself,'

'For crissake, Joe, I'd have to call you Sir, or even Mr President!'

'Or Mr Vice-President; sometimes these failed guys get the second slot,' Joe ventured.

Jeez, Ed thought, this fella doesn't miss a trick.

'Joe, that's like being redundant and being paid as well. Go for the big one!' Ed felt cornered and was angling for an exit. He saw Hal and waved him over.

'Joe, you haven't met Hal Whitehead, the Senator's cousin?'

'No, I haven't had the pleasure. Pleased to meet you, Hal.'

The two men then became engrossed in conversation and Ed Vince slipped away. Another glass of red was urgent. The Senator had been right. Joe was out for himself. All this 'if there is anything I can do' *was* hogwash!

Chapter Twenty-Nine

Three days before Christmas the US members of the Anglo-American fact-finding mission flew into Andrews Air Force base. As they hadn't suffered any hardship, the President was disinclined to make a public fuss, though a small reception would be given to satisfy press curiosity after they had first reported.

All three men were lean in their appearance and the tallest man, called Bill, was their spokesman. Eight chairs had been set out in the Blue Room. Three for the mission members and five for the President, the Chief of Staff, Harry Roberts, special advisor to the President, the Secretary of Defence and the Director of the CIA.

The President began with a brief word of welcome before calling on the Mission leader to report and he, in turn, acknowledged the friendly White House reception.

'Mr President, we have read your reports and we must say that the story of our being surrounded by a clutch of Saudi army vehicles is mistaken. Your overheads must have been confused with something else. Certainly there were a lot of children swarming round our trucks but that was all.

'We are sorry for the lack of communication. We were using a family well practised in the postal role. They were trustworthy, we were told, but clearly other loyalties won. It is difficult for us mere Westerners to penetrate the maze, even though we are Arabic-speaking.

'Regarding the lack of phone communication: we gave our word to avoid using mobiles and, indeed, to leave our vehicles switched off. So we had no way to charge the mobile batteries. We were treated so graciously that to be ungracious in the prohibitions that they asked seemed downright arrogant. And, of course, we thought you were getting our letters.

'Our Host, a most impressive man, had the complete respect of his tribe and followers and, I must say, had our respect as well. That, Mr President, is a brief summary. As a scientific and historical research team, we were shown much. That will be detailed in a written report. If you have any questions we will try to answer.'

'Thank you, Bill,' the President began. 'I would like to ask about the nature of your Host?

'He is man of profound stillness. Indeed, I feel unqualified to say more.'

'What did he say?' the President pressed.

'The uniting power of love was his constant theme and to pass our neighbour by denied that love. It was good to be in his presence. Perhaps that's why we stayed so long!'

'Did he say anything about the daily pattern of our life?'

'The law of love is written in our heart and we should listen to its promptings. There was much more, Sir, but I would need to ponder and remember.'

'What about security? Is he vulnerable?' The CIA Director asked.

'I was told he could detect agitated souls should they approach and he has a ring of dedicated guards. That's all I can say, Sir.'

'Four letters went astray, or was it five? Have you anything further to add?' the Director continued.

'It is difficult to say. As I have already said, the tribal loyalties are complex. But clearly there are orthodox religious factions who resent his presence. He has the ruler's protection and that, of course, is a powerful deterrent.'

Questions continued for some time, but Harry remained silent. Refreshments followed, after which selected members of the press were admitted, among them Joe Burns from the *Washington Post*.

The President and Harry Roberts didn't have the opportunity to discuss the fact-finding report until they were relaxing at Camp David at Christmas.

'I couldn't help thinking of the old grey-bearded man in the *Seven Pillars of Wisdom* "with a hewn face of great power and weariness". What wonderful language, Sir,' Harry mused.

'Yes, Harry, and those words, "The love is from God; and of God; and towards God."'

'A message for Christmas, Sir.'

'Be careful, Harry, or I'll twist some arms and make you Vicar of St John's.'

'Like the popular movie, that would be mission impossible!'

They both chuckled lightly.

'Camp David was a good idea, Sir,' Harry added. 'Mary appreciates it very much.'

'I'm glad. I suppose Sarah and I will face a media onslaught when we return.'

'Sarah's looking absolutely radiant, Sir. She's a very beautiful woman and her voice. It flows like liquid!'

'Harry, what she sees in this piece of faded history is a mystery!'

'Well, Sir, you have a certain poise!'

Both men burst out laughing.

'I wonder what Seb does over Christmas,' the President pondered. 'He lost his wife a long time ago but he never remarried.'

'I think he joins Jake Crystal and his family. He's a widower as well. I've got the feeling Jake has also caught the bug.'

'The location value bug?'

'Yes, but Jake, being in the newspaper business, is worried about being labelled partisan.'

'I wish more of them would think like that,' the President grumbled. 'Some of the papers read just like a party rag!'

They were silent for some time. The easy chairs were comfortable and the mood of contentment and wellbeing was tangible.

'Sir, this time last year I was driving you around in the limo...'

'Yeah, and I was taking out a special hazard insurance!'

'Seriously, Sir, I would like to thank you...'

'Harry, I would like to thank *you*. You were the only one who seemed to understand what happened on that walk-about. It was great support and just when it was needed'

'You can thank the Gulf for that.'

'Harry, I think we're being called to the table. I can see a beckoning hand!'

'Well, Sir, that's an order that we must not disobey.'

Chapter Thirty

Senator Sam Whitehead won the Iowa Caucus with ease and his nomination seemed assured. Smolensky was at the celebration, trying, as usual, to push the door open, but Whitehead wouldn't budge. So Joe was still out in the cold, but the chill didn't seem to get to him. For, come what may, he kept on pushing. Ed had to admire the guy, no wonder he'd created the Smolensky Corporation.

In many ways Joe had always got what he wanted, for he'd simply bought it. This was different, though; Whitehead wasn't up for sale but that made Smolensky even keener.

'When will that tycoon simply go away?' Whitehead grated.

'When you give him a job, Senator!' Ed answered.

'That'll be the day!'

Since returning from Camp David, the Press, as predicted by John Watson, had become obsessed with Sarah. Her beauty graced the front page of almost every daily and, being media-trained, she knew the way to sidestep questions without the slightest sliver of offence. Already her modest way of dressing had been named 'The Crawford Look', and the Picador-style hats she wore had overnight become a craze.

'Mr President, this is a good time to bury bad news,' Joss quipped, 'for Sarah has the front page to herself!

Duncan roared with laughter.

'Joss, trust you to think of that. No political opportunity ever escapes; no wonder you're my Chief of Staff!'

Joss smiled and sat back in the easy chair in the President's office.

'We still have no leads on the two security fellas.'

'The ones that Harry spotted?'

'Yeah, they're two bad eggs all right and the Feds are checking everything and I mean everything! They've checked out Smolensky!'

'And,' Duncan prompted.

'Clean, as white as the driven snow!'
'I've always thought his past...'
'Legit all the way!'
'That's a turn-up. It just shows how we colour things.'
'Well, he doesn't help. The way he swans around with heavies at his elbow.'
'Sam Whitehead was fooled as well.'
'I guess Joe was acting tough to show how good a party man he was. The sound Sam heard was probably passionate lies.'
'"Passionate lies," I've never heard that before.'
'Sir, you've had a sheltered youth!'
Duncan laughed.
'Seriously, Joss, do you think there's something out there? I've got to think of Sarah now.'
'Mr President, I don't know. The question is; whom have we upset? And if you believe the press, that's half the world! And home-grown stuff: well, nutters we will always have.'
They lapsed into silence for some time. Duncan watched his long-time friend, clearly deep in thought. They had come a long way. On the other hand, it seemed like yesterday when it all began.
Joss raised his head.
'It's election year, Sir. We need to think of a schedule. And Sir, there's Sarah. We also need to know your intentions.'
'Honourable, dad!' the President returned. 'Jeez, Joss, I never thought you'd ask me that one!'
'Seriously though, we'll have to know your plans.'
'You've got it.'
'The poll ratings haven't recovered yet. All that sniping about complacency has made its mark. Now, there's the anger at the 'incompetence' of the CIA. Some lawyer is actually claiming damages for the unnecessary anguish suffered by the families. Of course, Sir, it all rubs off on you.'
'I thought Sarah would have lifted things.'
'She has, but not enough. Her popularity isn't rubbing off!'
'My God, I'll have to have a face-lift!'
'Mr President, do you take anything seriously?'
'Yeah, the weather forecast.'
Joss laughed until the tears ran down his face.
'Well, Sir, apart from the weather forecast, can we agree that the re-election of John Duncan as President of the United States is also important? I certainly think it is.'

'This John Duncan fella, what's the big deal?'

'John Duncan's a big deal because he doesn't think he's a big deal. But the principles and the standards that he holds: they're the big deal!'

'Joss, you've hit the button. All this hard-nosed political stuff you've been plugging is a smokescreen! You're right, my friend, we need to set the course for the new year and we need to be ready when the time appointed nods. Joss, apart from the morning's programme, is there anything else I need to know about?'

'Harry's meeting the "Three Wise Men", as I call them. That is, Seb, Ed, and Leo. And Sir, Sarah's coming for lunch!'

'That, I'd not forgotten.'

There was a knock and Harry put his head round the door.

'Sorry to intrude, Mr President, but I thought you'd both like to know that Jake Crystal is joining us this morning.'

'So Seb's prevailed at last,' Joss responded.

'Well, Harry, Jake's a large publisher and in the world of ideas a friend like that is useful,' the President said knowingly. 'So, the three wise men are four!'

'Mr President, Seb would have it thirty-four, but I told him "Move the compass slowly."'

'I see you have your theme song ready!'

'But who will I commission for the music?'

'There you've got me.'

They laughed and Harry took his leave. His guests were due.

Chapter Thirty-One

The South Carolina and Nevada primaries were days away, but with an incumbent President going for his second term and with the unassailable lead of Sam Whitehead as the GOP front-runner, interest in the primaries was almost academic. Indeed, in a sense, the main election battle had begun. Joss had been pressing him to visit the New England States. He had little enthusiasm for the tour, but he knew he had to show his face. Of course, once over the initial inertia, he also knew he would enjoy the interchange and banter with the people. Anyway, it was a chance to press his questions and to bring the moral factor into focus.

His three questions, and indeed the whole idea of a new direction, had sunk without trace into pumpkin pie at Christmas. He needed a re-launch. The quick-fire exchanges of the tour were useful but he needed something more substantial and, in a sense, apolitical. There was the State of the Union coming up at the end of January, but somehow it wasn't the venue for what he had in mind, at least, not yet. The State of the Union was too high-profile too soon, and with its potential for contention inappropriate for the occasion.

The solution came as if by chance during a brief meeting with Harry's 'wise men'. Jake Crystal, at first a tentative participant, had become enthusiastic. It transpired that he was a founder member of a group of publishers who held a dinner in New York about this time.

'Our guest list often includes both Democratic and Republican Senators, so, Sir, it can be quite a party. Now this may be way off the screen, I mean way off! But I was wondering if you would honour us...'

'Jake, you're a gift from heaven, for the venue that I'm searching for is exactly what you've offered. Yes, subject to all the bits and pieces. The answer's yes, I would be delighted. *Alea iacta est* – the die is cast!' Harry smiled; the President liked his Latin aphorisms.

*

Jake had not been exaggerating. It was quite a party and the conversation was stimulating. Duncan knew all the Senators well, intelligent men, he had always judged. Good old Jake had shipped the goods. By tradition the members avoided a top table setting and the President's aides raised no objection.

'I'm just one of the fellas. I like it!' the President joked.

Of course, the deferential approach to the person of the President was not forgotten and the Secret Service presence was a strong reminder that the nation's chief executive was amongst them. The press were present, as were the cameras, so it wasn't quite their usual scene. Nevertheless, an atmosphere of informality was preserved. Eventually it was time to speak and after some warm and appreciative words from the acting chairman, the President stood up. There was no teleprompt or any of the trappings.

'Ladies and Gentlemen, this is just an excuse to re-launch the three questions I posed at the one-to-one before Christmas and which subsequently melted with the ice cream. You may remember: what is location value, who creates it, and to whom does it belong? That's it, that's the plug; in fact, questions for us all. I'm offering no answers, for answers close the door; I want to keep this door wide open. Well, folks, that's the commercial; now for the address, which I aim to keep as brief as possible.'

The President paused and for a moment stood quite still. Jake, watching from another table, noticed how he brought the dining room to rest. It was impressive.

'Publishing, I would suggest, is a touchstone of the nation's mental vigour. It is an important pivot of discrimination, with the bottom line pulling in one direction and the publisher's natural instinct pulling hard the other way. Clearly a balance is necessary. None of you are charities and none of you, I hope, are purely mercenary. Indeed, your role as diviners of the nation's literary talent is one of immense responsibility, for your choices are the mental food the nation savours. What you accept and what you reject counts, not just for your house, the author involved, but also for the community as a whole. None of us, I'm sure, would feed our children rubbish when good food is available. Books are food.

'No doubt our publications should reflect our basic democratic principles, but democracy is not perfect. In my opinion, it is fatally flawed, if it does not call upon the name of excellence. Excellence is the leaven, the drawing force that pulls our differing opinions to a common aspiration.

'Think of the works of Emerson: they were published. Think of the works of Jefferson. Indeed, our library shelves are weighed down by excellence. Yet there's the need, and here I'm quoting my good friend Harry Roberts. "We need to find new ways to say the old eternal things."'

The President smiled, pulling out a small volume from his inside pocket.

'An English friend gave this to me and, as you can see, it's a slim volume. Now this suits me just fine, for I'm not a speed-reader like JFK and, as you can probably guess, I have official papers to peruse. Can I impose upon you with a brief reading, for I feel it is so apposite to the modern need? Here it is.

To begin and maintain great popular movements, it is the moral sense rather than the intellect that must be appealed to, sympathy rather than self-interest. For however it may be with any individual, the sense of justice is with the masses of men keener and truer than intellectual perception, and unless a question can assume the form of right and wrong it cannot provoke general discussion and excite the many to action.'

'This was written by an American. He was a best seller and his books are still selling. His name was Henry George. The volume contains some of his *Gems*.' He held it up again. Like all good orators, he had a theatrical instinct.

'Ladies and gentlemen, yours is a noble profession. I salute you!'

Jake had been fascinated throughout. No speechwriter had written that. It was off the cuff, from the heart. Jeez, where does it come from? The President took his seat. It was a short speech, as he had promised and, for Jake, its very brevity made it powerful. All were on their feet, including him. All were applauding. Somehow John Duncan had captured the mood of the evening. He had reminded publishers about the obligations of their trade and had complimented their profession.

'That was a statesman's speech,' Jake's guest, a Republican Senator, stated roundly. 'It's so refreshing to be free of political point scoring.'

*

Joe Smolensky had been watching Duncan's speech on his hotel room TV. One of the old established companies he had recently bought was a publisher. A good deal, Joe thought. These old crusty firms always had prime sites. Joe took another swig of brandy, but he felt uncomfortable. His heart was pumping hard. Suddenly there was searing pain. He sat up rigid. Slowly he put the brandy down. 'Jeez, is this it?' he wheezed. Then the trouble passed.

Chapter Thirty-Two

The report of the President's speech at the publishers' dinner was too late for the early editions but not for breakfast news. Duncan, in his hotel suite flicked through the channels where comments seemed to be generally neutral. The busy intellectuals hadn't had their muesli yet, he thought cynically. He was about to press the remote, when the figure of Joe Smolensky was shown entering a clinic.

The presenter's commentary was one of breaking news of some significance.

Last night Joe Smolensky, President of the Smolensky Corporation, was admitted to an exclusive Manhattan clinic with a suspected heart problem. Fortunately no serious heart damage was suffered. Mr Smolensky was interviewed this morning as he left.

The screen now featured a smiling Joe engulfed by news reporters and media cameras.

Guys, I've had a gentle warning from the Boss and when he gets in touch you can't lie. So here it is straight, OK. I was sipping my favourite brandy and watching the President speak at a publishers' dinner, when the call came. I thought it was the big one, but it passed and here I am.

What was it, Joe, too much brandy or too much President? A reporter questioned above the clamour.

As I said, when the Boss calls, you tell it straight. It's the brandy, I guess, for I liked the President's speech. Yeah, it was good. But here, I'm still a Republican!

Joe then told them he would be having further tests.

The heart's too busy, they tell me. I can't pronounce the name but they assure me they can sort it out. OK, guys.

Suddenly Joe disappeared into his limo and was off.

'Well, well, Joe's suddenly realized he's mortal', Duncan mused.

There was an urgent-sounding knock and Billy Benson entered.

'Did you see that, Mr President? That's the best plug you've had,' Benson burst out in his quick-fire New York accent.

'You're not exaggerating, Billy?'

'No, Sir, that fella's well liked in the street. He speaks the language!'

'Billy, what did you think of the speech at the dinner? You never told me!'

'A bit short, Sir.'

The President exploded with laughter. It was so typical of Billy.

'If you don't watch out I'll hire Joe as my Press Officer!'

Billy laughed briefly. His mind was much too busy with plans and schedules.

'So what is it, Billy? Back to the bird, then another day up here in New England and then the Cottage?'

'That's it, Sir.'

Back at the White House with the morning papers, Duncan felt as if he hadn't been away. But the headlines soon reminded him. They seemed particularly trivial. 'Pompous President Pontificates:' 'Mr President, the three questions have been answered – your time *is* up!' 'Duncan, the undemocratic Democrat.' This wasn't reporting: it was a PR comedy.

The more substantial press were reasonable but lacking in their covering of the spirit he was trying to convey. Not a word about the quotation. No jibe about the 'has-been' George. The burning question: had his re-launch worked? Maybe Billy was right. Maybe Joe had given him a magic push? His comments were on everybody's lips. Much stranger things had happened.

The door opened. It was Joss with the morning's schedule.

'That talk you gave to Jake's people was good. I've got the feeling it went down well.'

'You wouldn't think that if you read the press!'

'Mr President, you did OK. I pick it up from the fellas here. When you do well, they talk. And when you don't, they don't! This morning they talked. Anyway, Joe gave you a plug. He's monopolized the screen this morning.'

'Yeah, Billy's big on that.'

'Mr President...' Joss hesitated.

'What is it, Joss?' Duncan knew the sound.

'Greed in high places, confidential information bought; it could hurt us, if it comes out. If we could delay?'

'No goddam deals, no cover-ups!'

'It's been stirred up deliberately.'

'Maybe, but high office means high responsibility. These things screw me up as much as you. I hate to see a guy ruin himself and his family.'

'Who is it?'

'Karl Deegir III.'

'Jeez, tell him to resign immediately. What got into him? The guy's loaded. How much?'

'Five million, a real estate deal: he could have taken a lot more.'

'Explain that to the ghettos!'

'God, how I hate this sort of thing, and his wife's such a delightful person!'

'I know, Joss, you're a human being. But Karl must resign – today! I'm sorry, that's the way it is. You may think I'm a hard bastard, but Joss, you've told the President and the President must act.'

'It's OK, Sir. I'd do the same if I were sitting in your seat. Thank God that's over, I hardly got a wink of sleep last night!'

'That's Joss, and that's why you're my Chief of Staff. My advice, do it now, ring Karl now. Delay won't help!'

'I know. There's another thing...'

'It's one of those mornings.' Duncan interjected. 'OK, shoot!'

'We're thinking of changing the White House security screening rules and we'll need your signature.'

'OK, see me when it's drawn up.'

Joss Johnson's footfall was heavy as he left, but Duncan did not have the slightest doubt that his friend's first phone call would be Karl.

'Karl, what a foolish thing to do,' Duncan mused. But then, community value dressed up as real estate trawled huge temptations in its wake. Here was the seedbed of corruption. Development plans revealed before their date of publication promised instant fortune. It was a bit like leaving children in a candy shop and then chastising them for gluttony.

Duncan felt even more determined. The three questions were all too current.

*

The resignation news had broken and the press were howling. Billy Benson was battling hard and under growing pressure. Billy knew the signs too well, a kind of blood lust, and he knew he had to call the President.

Things were almost out of hand when Duncan took the podium. There was an immediate lull.

'This morning at eight thirty the President was told of the misconduct of Karl Deegir's office. He was asked to resign immediately and this he did. All the relevant information relating to the unfortunate affair will be made available as soon as possible. There will be no cover-up!'

'We've heard all this before, Mr President!' a reporter shouted.

'Yeah, and you howled, and rightly, when smooth words were given as the answer. Here there are no back-door deals. The cards are on the table. And ladies and gentlemen of the press, how many of us here could do the same and walk away without a blush? Karl Deegir, I'm sure, will be his own worst critic. There will be punishment in plenty. So let's not crucify him and his family. *Now* do you see the importance of the questions! What is community value? Who creates it? To whom does it belong? I'll add another. What happens when that value can be claimed as real estate? These are real questions, questions for us all.

'Ladies and gentlemen of the press, that's it, OK?'

Chapter Thirty-Three

For three days the Karl Deegir affair dominated the media. The Republican-leaning press, of course, made the most of it. The President's ratings fell, but not as much as Joss had feared. Duncan's prompt action and his spirited offensive at the press briefing had stopped an all too possible slide in public confidence. Even so, it was a blow he could have done without. His re-launch, though, had worked and had been boosted by events that, on first reading, either seemed adverse or wholly unexpected. Joe Smolensky's close call bred an honest boost. Again a near to disastrous press briefing had been converted to an asset and a vehicle for his purpose. The three questions were now implanted firmly in the nation's mind. Yet their maintenance needed constant effort. There was, of course, a growing opposition as vested interests grew to see the fable they derided as an actual threat.

Harry Roberts, who had been 'camp following' Seb Sebbson on his speaking engagements, viewed this general overt opposition with concern, for it had an orchestrated feel. There were those who take and take, and only give in order to take more. They smile with surface charm, yet underneath are coldly ruthless. Harry knew such people could be dangerous when they felt their will was threatened, so he watched, not from the platform or top table, but the sidelines, as it were. It was always difficult to read, but for Harry, one thing was clear: opposition was vocal and growing.

Most of Seb's engagements were after-dinner occasions. He was hugely entertaining and on demand. Yet Seb didn't rush around. He couldn't. His body wasn't up to it. Lately, and Harry felt mistakenly, he had accepted platform engagements which were open to the public. These did not suit his style and it exposed him to a thuggish element in the hall; indeed, on one occasion it was clearly orchestrated.

Harry cautioned Seb to avoid such venues, but he, the old

corporate tiger that he was, was slow to take advice. One evening he was hit by a half-empty beer can as he left the hall, but it only seemed to make him more determined. Yet Seb still moved the compass slowly. He gauged his audience well and always kept his message humorous. Harry was concerned. Without doubt, the disruption was deliberate, but no one other than the President, or perhaps Joss Johnson, could bar him from the halls.

*

'You were masterly at the briefing the other morning, John. In fact, you faced a howling mob,' Sarah said softly, snuggling up to Duncan as they sat together after dinner.

'I'm an old pro, Sarah. Mind you, I don't blame the press. Thank God they do howl and are allowed to howl. Corruption at the top is awful. It undermines everything.'

'I sense a despondent note. Is there something troubling, or am I allowed to ask?'

'It's this constant sniping and mindless opposition. I've only posed three questions, for heaven's sake!'

'Yes, John, but most have got the message, especially those who've got their trotters in the trough!'

'I like it.' He laughed. 'It's good – trotters in the trough.' He laughed again. 'Sarah, it's time we were married or at the very least engaged.'

She snuggled closer.

'I thought you'd never ask! But John, you'll be accused of using your marriage as an election weapon.'

'Better have it over quickly then. How about Easter? And we could get engaged tomorrow.'

'John, you're being reckless.'

'It's an open secret, dear. It's time you were First Lady, and if we do the job at Easter you'll have six months at least.'

'There's that despondent note again!'

'Sarah, dear, my second term is far from certain. The Deegir case will rumble on. God knows what *it* will reveal. And the moral element that I've pressed is being ridiculed. Then there's the after-taste from the so-called hostage crisis. And, Sarah, people shout for change, but when it comes they shy away. Just like now. Opposition is hardening.'

'Well, Mr President, I'm going for a second term!'

'At least I've got one vote.'

'You haven't. I'm supposed to be an English rose!'
Duncan chuckled.

'Where's Harry? I haven't seen him for a day or so.'

'He's with Seb, trying to rein him in! Seb was hit by a beer can the other night and Harry wants to stop him appearing on platform venues, but the old fire-eater isn't used to taking orders. So Harry wants me to speak.'

'Will you?'

Duncan nodded reflectively.

'You're right, Sarah, I am feeling a bit down at present. The open awareness I felt on my 'disappearance' is fading. But,' he added mischievously, 'Easter will restore it!'

'I didn't say that I approved!'

'That's OK. I'll simply issue an executive order!'

The image of the smiling President and his lady flashed round the world. The expected news was official. Profiles, even supplements, listing Sarah's history were numerous. The London heavies had a field day when even the chattering class element was complimentary. For the moment they'd forgotten their Jane Austen jibes. Sarah had expected it, but the sheer pressure of it all was almost claustrophobic. She was seeing the media circus from the other end and with a vengeance.

The next day it was the Deegir case again. Obsession was the only word that she could find for it.

'They didn't heed you, John, they *are* crucifying him!' Sarah said at lunch.

'I've a mind to pardon him, but I can't, of course. It's that damned tycoon I'd like to nail. He knew Karl's family weakness: real estate, and by God he used it. The family own some nice stuff, not Manhattan but real attractive property in New England. Anyway, the tycoon's being questioned and he'll be a Republican, just to make it awkward. By the way, we had a very nice letter from Sam Whitehead. He told me he went to see Joe Smolensky in hospital. He says Joe had changed and felt his first alarmist fears had been mistaken.'

Duncan sat back in his seat. He had ten minutes before it started up again. Then it hit him. Smolensky was a multi-billionaire, yet he was a man of the people. They liked him and he could pull the votes. If Joe had really changed, Sam Whitehead might be tempted to offer him VP. Jeez, the change would need to be Damascene!

'John, what's wrong?'

'A scenario that I wish I hadn't thought of. Fears and imaginations, dear, but this Latin aphorism has a better hue.'

'Tell me.'

'Ex umbris et imaginibus in veritatem.'

'Veritatem is to do with truth. *Imaginibus* with imaginings, I suppose, and *umbris* shade.'

'Top of the class, my love. 'From shadows and appearances into truth.'

'You like Latin aphorisms, I hear.'

'Yes, it helps to preen my ego!'

Sarah laughed.

Chapter Thirty-Four

Billy Benson rushed up the corridor from the press-room, dashed past the secretaries, firmly knocked the Oval Office door and hurried in.

'What's wrong, Billy?'

'Mr President, Seb's been shot!'

'Is it...?'

'No, Sir,' Benson anticipated. 'The hospital says he'll survive!'

'My God, this opposition is for real! Billy, ask when Seb can have visitors. Sarah and I will go as soon as they allow. What hospital?'

'Somewhere between here and Baltimore.'

'Where's Harry?'

'At his bedside.'

'Good.'

'Is there anything else?'

'A crude note, Sir – a marker pen on newspaper. It said "S(lo) b, shut up!" This is it, Sir,' he added, handing over his telephone note.

'Crude, OK, but to the point!'

'How should I handle the press' Sir?'

'Billy, you're good at this. Emphasize the attack on free speech, free enquiry and discussion. Ask the question: What are you afraid of, Mr Big? Billy, the fella who left the note wasn't a wino!'

'Got it, Sir!'

Benson quickly left and Joss was next.

'Billy's told you?' Joss said briefly.

Duncan nodded.

'I have alerted security, Mr President. Thank God we got rid of those two guys!'

'What are you trying to tell me Joss?'

'There's something big out there. Someone doesn't like us messing.'

'With what, Joss?'

'One guess, Sir – real estate!'

'Why are the baddies the only ones to get the message?'
'Good question, Sir!'
'Joss, this tycoon who tempted Karl into trouble, we need the Feds to make it special. I've been reading about him. He makes Smolensky look a wimp. Glit Jones is the name! A rock star once, made a pile and stuck it into land.'
'Where else?'
'The Wedding, Mr President, we'll need to have a lengthy session. Half the world will be knocking. It's a security nightmare!'
'Why can't we keep it private and have it at St John's?'
'It's the National, Mr President, for you're the President!'
'So I'm told! Well, Joss, you're in charge, for you're best man.'
'You didn't tell me!'
'Did I have to? Joss, I don't want a fuss at the hospital. See what you can do.'
'Seb will like it.'
'Yeah, but the doctors must agree.'
' Got it.'

Security kept the Press at bay and with the briefest of waves the President and Sarah entered the Hospital. At the reception Duncan repeated his plea for simplicity. He was visiting a friend and it was private. Indeed, the whole visit was achieved without fuss and although some were curious and overtly so, decorum wasn't breached.
Seb was heavily sedated but he was obviously pleased.
'Seb, the doctors say you're doing fine. Rest well, my old friend,' Duncan whispered in his ear. 'We'll have you out in no time.' Then after watching him for a few moments, the President briefly took his hand and left. On the way out Duncan was more forthcoming but it was quick and brief. Harry was waiting in reception.
'Do you need a lift, Harry?' the President asked easily.
Sarah was impressed. It was all so ordinary. What a contrast from the usual razzmatazz.
'Yes, Sir, I came by train and taxi.'
Inside the well-upholstered air-conditioned interior, it was suddenly quiet.
'Seb was lucky!' The President almost whispered.
Harry nodded.
Sarah sensed Harry's sombre mood and guessed his thoughts

were raising memories of the Gulf, but she said nothing.

'This wasn't a hobo, Harry. The note left was too clever!'

'Yeah, someone out there thinks his empire's threatened, I don't know why, for in Seb's case he didn't push at limits. As we keep saying, Seb moved the compass slowly. I sense an obsessed mind.'

'Anything more, Harry?'

'Well, Sir, it's sheer speculation, but I've got a hunch this being's a reclusive. He's not a Joe Smolensky joking with the fellas!'

Involuntarily, Duncan's mind turned to the billionaire Glit Jones, but he held his peace.

The limo glided through the dark wintry streets like some sleek animal. In fact, the Presidential motorcade was more like a carrier task force with the Secret Service vehicle in the front and another in the wake, and with the outriders, like destroyers busy sweeping here and there. Inside the limo it was quiet.

'Harry, are you busy tonight?' Duncan asked impulsively.

'Nothing fixed, Sir.'

'Yeah, but I bet Mary has you on a line!'

'True, Sir, she was thinking of her favourite spaghetti place, but nothing's booked.'

'Do they do take-aways?'

'For the White House, Mr President, they'd bring the kitchen over!'

Duncan chuckled briefly.

'What do you think, Sarah?'

'It's a great idea. I know the place. Mary and I have been a number of times. Italian, and very friendly.'

'Let's do it.'

Sarah was struck, once more, by the simple nature of it all. Four friends were having a take-away. The trappings of power had been suspended, but they were there and waiting. One phone call and the idyll would dissolve.

The President and Harry were relaxing on the sofa, sipping dry white, while Sarah and Mary were setting up the table in anticipation of the take-away. The two men had been quiet for some time. Neither man was given to unnecessary chatter.

'Harry, have you ever heard of Glit Jones?' Duncan suddenly asked.

'Strummed a guitar some years ago, I remember. Didn't stick

it long but put his windfall into property, I believe.'

'That's him. He's the one who tempted poor old Karl. The Feds are on to him, but he's covered his tracks and it's lawyers all the way to Christmas! Maybe you could take a peek. Jones, apparently, has quite a pad.'

Harry nodded pensively.

'Palaces in the midst of slums,' he murmured.

'What was that, Harry?'

'Palaces in the midst of slums,' the big man repeated. 'Jones is mega rich; too much wealth corrupts if it isn't used to ease the need of others.'

'Harry, that's a powerful image. Remind me to plagiarize it some time!'

Roberts burst out laughing.

'Ah, here's the take-away, we're in business,' Duncan noted while getting to his feet. 'It smells real good. Mary's looking very dainty and attractive. Have you set the date yet?' he added.

'Some time after you, Sir: Mary's angling for the President and the First Lady to attend!'

'The little devil!' Duncan chuckled.

Supper proceeded in a light-hearted and easy way. Then halfway through the meal the President paused and focused purposefully on his secretary.

'Mary, Sarah would like you to be her bridesmaid. Would you be willing to oblige?'

The blood suddenly drained from Mary's face.

'Mary, I'm not sending you to the pen!'

Harry's humour bubbled. The President had already hinted some few days ago.

'I never dreamt. What an honour, but, Sir, my knees would knock; I'd disrupt the service!'

'Yeah, they'd sound well in the National!'

'The National, it's so big! God!'

'Mary, you've met the greatest in the land and in other lands, my dear. You'll be fine.' Duncan paused. 'Mary, you're keeping us hanging out there!'

'Yes, Sir, of course, Sir,' she said, her voice emotional, and tears began to trickle. Responding, Sarah rose up and in a single movement took her hands and embraced her.

'Joan will be matron of honour. So you'll have support,' she said softly.

'Oh, that's good,' Mary reacted.

'Glasses, everyone!' the President intoned. 'Would that all treaties were as easy!' Duncan joked.

Chapter Thirty-Five

It had been a wonderfully spontaneous evening. Mary was over the moon, yet Harry was disturbed; disturbed by the image of Seb lying helpless in hospital and the possible calculating will behind it; disturbed when he thought of the two rogue Gulf vets who'd been included in the White House detail; indeed, disturbed that the investigators were running blind. With the wedding coming up, and fast, it had all the ingredients of a security nightmare.

Who was this Glit Jones? The net described him as a developer and art collector. There were architectural models of projected schemes, but nothing Harry would have thought of as mega, for he'd visualized vast complexes. Another illusion shattered. Well, the President wanted him to take a peek and when the President spoke, you took a peek!

Harry Roberts knew he had come a long way in a short time, but he'd never flaunted his position and could still visit restaurants without being recognized. That luxury, though, was fading. Too many mug shots in the press, he grumbled to himself.

Limo travel was comfortable and tempting but Harry resisted it, preferring train and taxi. By doing that he felt much more in touch. Joss Johnson had told him that Jones had a pad in upstate Virginia. So Harry took the train.

The taxi man at Richmond spoke little English. He had a furtive look. A get-away driver in a 'B' movie, Harry thought with some amusement, but a few words in Harry's halting Arabic were enough to throw the switch. Out came a torrent, meaningless to Harry, but at least the driver joined the human race!

Harry bought the best map available and when he asked where Jones lived there was no hesitation from the locals. 'Glitterlane, but you can't get near it. He owns the land for miles around.'

The driver, now cooperative, obeyed the big man's every whim until they reached some high ground just outside the no-go area of the Jones estate. There they parked. Getting out, Harry scanned the area with his Special Service glasses, and there it was, partially hidden by trees, a perfect specimen of an old plantation mansion. Hearing footsteps, he spun round to discover a private security man. Typical nightclub heavy, he thought, with a designer beard. 'Private property, buddy. Move on!' the heavy barked. Harry could have cut him in two. Instead, he smiled politely and apologized.

A polite word from the heavy would have allayed suspicion but the obsessive habit of the master was implanted in the servant. Such was Harry's reading and, as far as the big man was concerned, Glit had made his first mistake.

They drove back to the local township, where Harry bought the driver a coffee. Casual enquiries from the waitress confirmed his speculations. He hadn't achieved much nor had he learned firm facts, but he'd got the message, the underlying feeling.

*

After listening to Harry, the President was quiet for some time.

'That fella could fund a carrier task force, and if Karl Deegir's anything to go by, God knows whom he's hooked and then polluted. Anyway, the Feds are onto him and the lawyers are making a killing. But, Harry, we can't put him in the slammer because he's an eccentric. The question is, did he finger Seb, and why for crissake? Dammit, it's all speculation, but it's too serious. We can't let it drift. Three questions! Why the earthquake?'

'It *is* an earthquake, Sir. The good see it as salvation, and the fearful as destruction. It's potent stuff.'

'But harmless when you move the compass slowly.' Duncan's smile was mischievous.

Harry made no response and stillness seemed to swallow sound.

'I know, you're thinking of Seb,' Duncan said quietly.

Harry nodded.

'It's OK. We'll not let this one go!'

They were in the Oval Office, it was well past six and the city's lights were blinking in a cold and watery night. The President was pensive and Harry sensed his need to talk, but his chief remained silent as if there were a struggling impulse yet to manifest. Harry waited.

'I had another experience this morning, rather similar to that morning when I "disappeared." Seb lying there made me wonder if I were pushing things too hard. You know, truth before its time is dangerous. I had doubts, Harry, and they got to me. Why should I assume I knew the answers to the degradation that I see around me? I felt a phoney and it wasn't pleasant. Then I remembered something from my university days, something that I haven't thought about for years. It just popped in. The words of Socrates – *Knowledge is simply recollection*. The world lit up again. In a way my doubts were right, for knowledge knows, not Duncan! It gave me confidence, Harry, the heart to carry on. Am I kidding myself?'

'Sir, Socrates never kidded anybody!'

The President burst out laughing, so much so that tears began to trickle down his cheeks.

'Hey, there's a nice red in the private office cabinet. Let's have a glass!'

'As they say, I thought you'd never ask.'

'Thanks for that, Harry. You know, this job ain't easy at times!'

Harry said nothing. What could he say? The Presidency was an awesome responsibility.

Chapter Thirty-Six

For the President the wedding was a kaleidoscope of concerns and emotions. The natural human joy of finding a companion such as Sarah was paramount. Agonizing over security, though understandable, was a perpetual distraction. The experts, or professional pessimists as he branded them, brimmed with nightmare possibilities. In the end all that he could do was trust.

Envy and even hate spilled into the columns of some clever dailies, but the overwhelming response was one of celebration. The marriage was a national event, a unifying force.

Sarah had no close family, but the expected presence of the Prince and Duchess and, of course, Sir James and Lady Babbington, made up for any sense of lack. Who wasn't on the guest list was the question, for heads of state from every corner of the globe would jostle in the National. Those intellectuals who saw the US in decline might see the gathering as a hollow show. Cautious minds, of course, would pause. America was hugely influential.

Much as he would have liked to separate the private from the public, Duncan knew his wedding day was not his own to play with as he would. He was the President. In the traditional sense he saw the occasion as Sarah's day, but in truth it was a public event. The office of President demanded it. Again he could not vaguely greet the many guests en masse. Each needed attention, for National pride was ever rampant.

Sarah was British. Understandably the British contingent received special attention and Harry Roberts, now known to most as a close confidant of the President, was their special escort. This the Babbingtons knew to be a compliment. Indeed, the Prince, sensing Harry's qualities, found the big man charming company.

Near the Cathedral the logistics slotted like a jigsaw. On the morning the limos were lined like centipedes along Wisconsin Avenue. No foreseeable aspect of security had been neglected. Inside the service proceeded.

Harry remained at the back, alert to every movement,

especially those that seemed contrived. There was nothing, and the ancient dignity of the service proceeded as expected. John and Sarah Duncan were man and wife, and the nation had a new First Lady.

Sarah, of course, was stunning, and tomorrow her wedding gown and every nuance of behaviour would be analyzed in print. And there was darling Mary, playing her part as ever with a total faithfulness; her bridesmaid's dress suited her, he thought; she looked quite tall.

Next was the reception at the White House. Here Harry felt much more content. It was home territory, as it were.

The President and Sarah were spending Easter at Camp David, but in truth the Chief Executive was never quite on holiday. Briefings would continue and phone calls would be numerous. Joss Johnson would keep the pack at bay, but events and circumstance waited for no man. That being so, propriety lent a certain measure. After all, it was the Easter break.

Now strengthened by a firm domestic base, Duncan felt new vigour urging him to press with his reforms. How could he proceed? How could he keep his oft-repeated questions from sinking to the level of a chat-show joke? How could he fire enquiry into what was generally thought to be a bloodless, tedious world of figures and statistics? He couldn't, thinking of the words he'd quoted at the publishers' venue. He needed to excite the people's innate sense of justice, and simply point out what was right and what was wrong. It was crassly wrong to walk by poverty on the other side and see it as the natural order. Smug complacency built on smug complacency and little else. Lazy, unemployable, quasi-criminal drop-outs, these were quick unthinking words of little meaning unless you saw the situation on the ground. He was President of all the people and pigsty squalor was no fit place to bring up human beings. Lenin's socialist arrogance and Mao's murderous inhumanity clearly hadn't provided the answers, but Henry George, a good home-grown American, *had*. Duncan was convinced. George had found the secret waiting quietly in nature and his book was but a simple revelation of the obvious. Such simplicity, though, was powerful. It could cut through steel, but in the oft-repeated words he now ascribed to Seb was the ever-cautionary injunction: move the compass slowly!

The immediate question still remained. How could he progress and keep enquiry fresh? Just as in sailing, a new tack was required against the constant and prevailing wind of plain indifference and inertia.

For the new First Lady there was no sudden rush to change the décor of the White House, and, even though she was media-trained, no attempt to seek the limelight. Duncan's admiration was confirmed. Taste was her mark, not fashion. In fact, her tasteful choice of clothes became the fashion. The fashion icons didn't like it, though they had the sense to keep their lips well sealed. However, snide asides escaped at times, revealing their disdain. Peddlers of undress, John Duncan labelled them. With her husband's approval she'd accepted being the patron of two established charities. That, so far, was the sum of her public commitments, apart from accompanying the President on his various outings.

After the busy media whirl, the relative calm of White House life was welcome. The truth was, Sarah was content and happy. The future would bring its roles and opportunities.

Seb had not been fit enough to attend the wedding at the National. Progress had been slow, but now a slimmer, nimbler Seb was climbing back to fitness. Jake and he had resumed their lunches at the Hay Adams, but now there was a Secret Service man in tow. Seb didn't like the fuss. Lightning didn't strike the same tree twice, he grumbled. Yet he accepted the security with a certain graciousness. It was the President's will and that for Seb was good enough.

His return to the circuit, as it were, was all Seb seemed to think about. He had a job to do, and no paid thug was going to stop him!

Harry Roberts knew that Seb would never walk on eggs for long. He needed to stride out. That was his nature. In the meantime he would do his best to calm down Seb's ambition.

Chapter Thirty-Seven

Harry Roberts and Mary were married two months later than the President, almost to a day. But whereas the President's marriage had been a national event, the marriage of his secretary to his special advisor was private and lacking almost totally in publicity. The guest list was small. Mary's family – her sister was bridesmaid. Harry's friends from his discussion group and here only six were able to attend. Harry's best man was an ex-SAS man he'd known in the desert, but the big man, being an army orphan, had no family. Then, of course, there was the President and First Lady: Mary had got her way, Harry joked afterwards with his Chief. Of course, Joss and Joan Johnson were amongst the few, along with some of Mary's White House secretary friends. It was as Mary had desired, a private wedding but with one special feature: the President had attended.

It was the first time that Duncan had met any of Harry's discussion group friends. They were, to a man – and woman, very ordinary and straightforward people. There were no airs or graces, no posturing, thank God, though some, understandably, were somewhat overawed at first. Duncan sensed a common thread, integrity you could take for granted. Reliable people, he concluded. He liked them.

Every move Glit Jones made was monitored, but every hint of corresponding harassment was listed by Glit's lawyers. Media men and column writers took his part; indeed, his popular defence was like a carrier task force wall of steel. Nothing could get through. Glit was clever, and the deft use of his many media contacts was masterly. This made the Feds obsessive, and so the game continued.

Watching from the sidelines, Harry felt that Jones rather liked the game. He was an oddball, that at least was certain, but nothing had been proved to link him with the crime against Seb

Sebbson. That linkage was a hunch; a Presidential whim backed up by the musings of a close advisor. The Deegir case had prized the lid, but Jones was resisting with uncommon skill. For Harry, the inner debate, the to-and-fro of yes and no, continued, but the feeling he had had remained. There was something very strange about the owner of the upstate mansion in Virginia. One day Glit would falter, miss an obvious move and so reveal himself. Meanwhile nothing, absolutely nothing, could be pinned on him, for he'd wriggled out of everything.

Opposition was growing, not only in an academic sense, but also in clever and dismissive jibes. Indeed, it seemed that prime-time chat-show hosts now felt themselves obliged to target the 'obsession' of their President. At least, it wasn't indifference, Duncan thought, but he knew the time had come to act. Then it struck him. He could use Harry's 'Palaces in the midst of slums' aside. No, 'Mansions in the midst of slums': the sound was better. Why do we walk by on the other side? Why the lack of sympathy, not the sentimental stuff, but the core human feeling for the suffering of others? Poverty *was* a moral issue.

Duncan sat back in his swivel chair. It was one thing to contemplate poverty from the comfort of his private office, or the bullet-proof cocoon of the presidential limo, but it was a wholly different thing to view the starkness of the problem face to face. The security boys would have kittens but he was resolved to visit the slum areas: an eyeball-to-eyeball confrontation.

For a month the President crisscrossed the country: from the Eastern Megalopolis to California; Chicago to Houston; the badlands where he found them and Miami in the south. The press were not informed of his itinerary. There was no plan. Nothing was checked out. In other words, it was spontaneous, and if Security were shell-shocked, the violent forces did not have prior notice. The President simply appeared and always at his side was Harry Roberts.

Although both men reported to the White House with reasonable frequency, their general absence was a strain on Sarah and on Mary, but, as Sarah said, they had married men, not mice, and that was that.

At first the media and press were scathing, seeing the whole thing as a publicity stunt and a crude one too, in view of the election. But, as the press did not know where Air Force One might land, this view was given the lie. Slowly opinion turned as local news reports revealed the nature of the President's progress. Some of the verbatim exchanges were bizarre.

'What's a dude like you want here?'

'Seeing what you need.'

'Listen, fella, I take what I need, OK. What's your goddam name?'

'I'm the President.'

'Son-of-a-bitch, yeah, I've seen your mug shot. Good to know ya, man!'

This short recording made a killing for the local TV station. It was repeated on prime time endlessly and cut the sniping of the clever intellectuals dead. Slowly, opinion in the mass of the people was changing. The moderator of a prestigious political panel actually started his session with the telling biblical quotation, *By their fruits ye shall know them*. This put the subsequent discussion in perspective. The President had put himself in the front line at no small danger. Some thought his actions irresponsible, while others argued the opposite, but all agreed that the President was practising what he preached. In plain-speaking terms, that was the bottom line.

Duncan had achieved what a week of speeches would have failed to do, but more was needed. Now was the time for rhetoric, the formulations that would mould his hopes of reformation. The questions remained, but now they needed to be aired with pointed reference to the inequalities eating at society's heart. How was location value relevant to an underclass of beings living at the edge? This wasn't easy to put in simple terms that all would understand, but stinging the rich *was* easy. This was the facile Marxist message, attractive to the underdog, but in the end it merely changed one set of fat cats for another.

The month was up. It was time for the routine of the White House and for Sarah. Now he needed a venue, a Jake Crystal apolitical kind of venue, but he didn't issue orders. Something, he felt sure, would happen.

Chapter Thirty-Eight

The Convention address at the end of August, although a party platform, was a major national event. Here, it was expected, Duncan would reveal his second term proposals, but that was over six weeks away. He needed some appropriate venue in the meantime, something to keep the pot simmering. Ten days had passed since his 'tour' had ended. Still he waited; he wanted something to arise, not an artificial Presidential fix. Then, almost when he'd thought he'd lost the opportunity, Seb produced the answer. A conference of School Principals set up by a friend of his. As usual, the solution had come right on the wire. Since his 'disappearance' he had noticed how precise this natural way of working was. Who or what informed such fine precision was a mystery. You waited, then an impulse came that carried life, and then you acted. An impulse, though, without that spark of life was useless. It was merely thinking.

The venue was an hotel in Bethesda, Maryland, just outside the DC border. No one knew who the dinner's 'surprise guest speaker' was, but when they saw the TV cameras and the media paraphernalia the noise of speculation rose. Security precautions gave a further indication, so when the President and First Lady arrived, surprise was well tempered by expectancy, but no one had dreamt the speaker was to be the President.

The buzz of conversation in the dining room rose in volume, but it settled as the meal progressed. There was a press presence, but invitations had been limited. Sarah recognized the faces, those in Billy Benson's better books.

Like the Jake Crystal occasion, the top table was round, and similar to all the rest. Duncan and Sarah both found the conversation fascinating. There were no awkward silences and the message was clear: Leave teaching to the teachers. Get Federal and State busybodies off our backs and curb the PC lobby.

It wasn't a gathering of pinkos, Duncan thought wryly, no wonder Joss was so uptight. 'If you speak to that bunch of neocons you'll alienate half the party,' he had barked. 'And if you go on like this,' he'd added, 'you'll end up like the Roman Gracchi, and those two guys came to one awful sticky end.' Joss had lost his cool but two minutes later he'd apologized. Yet Duncan could not find the will to compromise. In education, party political considerations were invalid.

Soon it would be time to speak, but what could he say to these good people other than to praise their stand? As usual, his mind seemed totally bereft of inspiration. He had a prepared speech at the ready, but it was useless. 'It's going to the wire again,' he thought. 'Jeez, this game of brinkmanship is something else!'

After the Chairman's humorous, yet respectful introduction, Duncan got to his feet. He scanned the dining room and the expectant sea of faces turned towards him. He opened his mouth and words came from where he knew not, but they came resonant and clear.

'Ladies and gentlemen, what can I tell you that you do not know already? I can only praise. I praise your devotion to the age-old principles that pass from generation to generation. I praise the measured discipline you instil and I praise the love and care you shower upon the children. We were all children once; even Presidents go through the process. We knew when teacher cared and we knew when teacher loved their subject. Folks, that is the limit of my presumption.'

The President smiled, gathering the attention of his audience.

'Recently I have visited some of the blighted areas that shame our cities. This you will have noticed in the press and media. It has been a salutary experience. Indeed, in such areas education has a whole new meaning. There were a number of things that struck me. One was the sudden change from soaring wealth to slum. It was mansions in the midst of misery and it happened suddenly, even in the space of a block. To repeat, mansions in the midst of misery: it was stark! Doubtless, we are all aware of this, but do we feel it? Perhaps we do, but the problem is so well established, so deep rooted. We're overwhelmed. What can we do? So we pass by on the other side. And worst of all, the causes of the problem lie unchallenged.

'Three questions have been posed: what is location value? Who creates it? And to whom does it belong? Recently a TV company conducted a questionnaire, with the majority finding that location value was community created. Now, if community created, to whom does it belong? Currently real estate law allows this value to be collected privately. It can be a tidy sum, indeed, a very tidy sum! Is this the cause of mansions in the midst of misery? A leading question, you may say, but if the goal is truth can it be invalid?

'Throughout history the Creator has been blamed for man's misfortunes, a convenient ploy, I would suggest, for those who've grabbed the cake. The Earth is bountiful, yet what is given to all ends up as an inequity of haves and have-nots. Surely nature can't be blamed for such stupidity!

'The crude experiments of the communist world spawned a murderous tyranny. They failed. Here, of course, the socialist mind-set has a user-friendly face that caters for the crying needs of welfare. In the short term this is both commendable and necessary, but I would suggest that a solution to the harsh inequities in our midst will be found, not just in welfare thinking, but also in those laws within the heart of nature. The questions are the key. The thirst for justice is the will. But we must tread carefully. Sudden harsh directives cannot be our way.'

The President breathed deeply as if garnering strength, and Sarah smiled encouragement, but her media-savvy heart was beating fast. John was pushing at the limits. Only God knew how the pressrooms would react.

'During my wanderings in these areas of poverty I saw boredom, bestial behaviour and belligerence. Who was the dude? they sneered, but when they learned it was the President, they changed. Some lit up. Humanity was awakened. Ladies and gentlemen, poverty is a curse. How dare we be indifferent?'

The light was fading as the limo nosed its way back from Bethesda. Inside it was quiet, the outside noises like a whisper.

'What happened in there this evening? Did I get through?' Duncan shook his head. 'The questions were very bland.'

'They're educationalists, John.'

'What did you think?'

'Short, but powerful. You were pushing at the limits, but you'll have to spell it out at the convention.'

'Joss won't like that.'

'No, but you're going for the bundle, as they say, and you've prepared the ground. Who knows what will happen'.

*

Chapter Thirty-Nine

Joss Johnson was very well aware that his friend the President was going for the bundle, as Sarah had put it. Since the morning of his 'disappearance' John Duncan seemed to shed all interest in the political cut and thrust. Indeed, there were rumblings in the party about their Chief's indifference, and if he mentioned Sam Whitehead, it was usually to say that he agreed with him. Billy Benson was having kittens daily and this morning wasn't an exception, with 'Mansions in the midst of misery' as an almost universal headline. Yet Johnson knew his friend had hammered home his point with unusual success. On the other hand, a powerful business alliance was ranged against him, their spokesmen being amongst the most respected in the land. Duncan's stance was un-American. The age-old dream of riches in the land of opportunity was being eroded, for if Duncan had his way all would be scythed to uninspiring stubble.

The next morning Leo Pucci countered with a stinging article, which was echoed by Ed Morrison. Harry's 'wise men' had sprung to the President's defence. The uninspiring stubble was a socialist projection that had no resonance with the President's intention. Even so, the polls didn't make good reading and pundits were beginning to predict a victory in November for the GOP. Yet Duncan didn't seem to be concerned. In fact, Joss felt his Chief had grown fatalistic. Joss was frustrated but he knew that there was little point in trying to change the President's direction. Hope, however, was not dead, for John had that uncanny knack of extracting the proverbial rabbit from the hat.

*

Duncan was well aware of the election uncertainty and he also sensed the staff's irrational faith that somehow he would pull if off. He wasn't indifferent, but at times he felt himself to be a curious onlooker wondering how the dice would fall. As for the questions and the direction of his policy, Duncan was resolved.

There'd be no wavering when it came to natural principles. How could there be? How could he ignore self-evident fact for petty short-term gain? Too easily politics became a blind-man's game of self-deception.

*

The Republican camp was no longer cautious in their optimism. Ed Vince bubbled daily with photo opportunities and PR possibilities. The September convention was billed as if it were the Second Coming. But Ed was frustrated with the candidate, for the Senator refused point blank to take a swipe at Duncan. It was unnatural, he complained openly, but Sam Whitehead only smiled at Ed's predictability.

'When a man tells it straight, it's foolish to attack him, and, Ed, we're winning!'

Ed cast his eyes towards the heavens but said no more.

'Where's Joe?' the Senator asked.

'Out on the streets whipping up support. He thinks he's the goddam VP!'

'Is Hal with him?'

'Yeah.'

Whitehead nodded. Joe was popular. Hal had confirmed it more than once. The blue-collar workers liked him.

*

The two questionable Gulf veterans, who'd been employed briefly by White House security, had been investigated thoroughly and Harry's intervention justified. A full internal investigation was under way at the Pentagon, as the softly-softly approach had been abandoned. How had such a potentially dangerous error occurred? Bribery was an obvious suspicion, but the danger of an innocent man being fingered was a powerful restraint. And, of course, the whole thing could have been an error.

It was during a casual conversation with Joss Johnson that Harry, still suspicious of Glit Jones, asked the question. It was sudden and spontaneous and it had the note of credibility. Was anyone in the relevant Pentagon department a collector? We were all hung up on various trivialities, but obsession-blinded. Indeed, the only safe obsession was the truth!

Joss smiled knowingly when Harry spoke.

'It's an obvious linkage, but I never thought to ask the question.

I wonder if the spooks checked it out? What's the betting that they didn't? Jeez, Harry, I'm glad you're not after me!'

For a time both men sat quietly pensive.

'Are they in this evening?' Harry questioned casually.

'No, they're at the Embassy, I mean the British Embassy, and an informal dinner I believe.' Joss smiled. 'The Brits are taking over and John's probably offering the new term VP job to Roger Blackstone. Good old Zac, our long-suffering friend, wants a rest!'

Harry laughed.

'The President and the First Lady are so well suited.' It was almost a whisper.

'Yes, it's been a blessing.' Then Joss added quietly, 'Will we make it in November?'

'It will go to the wire. It always does with the President. But this isn't an ordinary election.'

'Jeez, you don't have to tell me, Harry. Poor old Billy Benson tears his hair out daily and I completely lost my cool, but it makes no difference. He's going for it and no one's going to run him off the course. Mind you, I agree with him, and by heavens he's prepared the ground. Even so, it ain't politics. The people expect some party fireworks, not a love-in!'

'I wonder, we may be in for a surprise.'

'But not the one we want, according to the pollsters!'

'I still wonder! – Joss, I just don't know. My hunch still stands though. We'll not know until we hit the wire.'

'One thing, Harry: he'll have to make one helluva Convention speech.'

'He will! You know, I went to that School Principals' thing the other night. Seb got me a ticket and I sat with Billy Benson and Joe Burns from the *Post*. The President's opening was brilliant. 'What can I tell you that you don't know already?' It got their sympathy immediately and it was true. Then he praised their better parts. Teach by praising. He got his point across without a hint of preaching. He told me afterwards that he'd had no idea what he was going to say. In fact, he couldn't formulate anything before he spoke, but when he opened his mouth out it came. It's high risk, but it's hugely effective, for it's tailored to the moment. It may be not high rhetoric but by God it hits the button. Billy Benson was grumbling, as he does, but he had to admit he carried them to a man. And, Joss, he'll do it again at the Convention - you'll see, he'll carry the hall.'

'Yeah, and they'll carry me out! The suspense will be too much!'

Harry chuckled.

'He's never been the same since his morning's "disappearance",' Joss continued. 'Before that I could always figure him out. Now he shoots off at a moment's notice and I must admit he's almost always right. Harry, what happened that morning?'

'Only he could answer that. My hunch is that reason married with the heart.'

'I wish I knew what you mean, but it sounds right.'

'He's loath to waste time on pointless politicking. Mind you, he's politically aware. Politics is still the art of the possible, and tempering remedy with reason is an art.'

'Thanks for that, Harry. It seems to me we've got a President who is present!'

Harry's smile was just discernible.

Sarah knew the President's close friends well: Joss and Joan, and Harry and Mary, but there were a host of others and, of course, there were the White House staffers. It was a steep learning curve, but, being journalist-trained, she had a facility for placing people. It was just as well: as the First Lady, she had to watch her word and step. As they said stateside, people took offence real easy. There were also the numerous agencies whose representatives came and went with frequency. The Presidency was demanding and time put limits on the sum of things the President could do. Often he had to make the choice between conflicting experts. He had to be a listener, but also have a strong and independent mind that wasn't easily swayed. Thank God JFK had been of that ilk during the Cuban missile crisis.

The issue of location value he saw as fundamental. Real estate law had plundered the community fund and tax had plundered individual and corporate earnings. It was, he grumbled, the economics of the madhouse.

'But, Sarah,' he had added. 'We think the madhouse is reality and in changing that Job's patience is a first necessity.'

At that moment Sarah felt a new devotion to the man she'd married. She had stumbled into something rather rare. Sometime in the future she would tell him, but not just now.

Chapter Forty

Two weeks before the Democratic Convention, news broke that Glit Jones had been found dead beside the broken remains of a priceless vase, one of his most prized possessions. A heart attack brought on by shock was said to be the cause. Armed with the necessary clearance the FBI were on the scene immediately, to find a treasure trove of documents beyond their wildest dreams. Jones, the obsessive collector that he was, had kept everything and, like the Nazis, everything was recorded. The spider's web of conspiracy and corruption took the hardened lawmen's breath away. Immediately the FBI Director requested a meeting with the President.

Joss Johnson's step was heavy as he made his way to the President's private office. This was the hammer blow, the *coup de grace*, and just ten days before the Convention. The timing couldn't be worse, for all would be blamed on Duncan's lax administration.

Joss knocked gently and went in.

'What's wrong, Joss? Is it World War III?'

'Pretty close, Sir!'

Joss went on to explain the situation and all the ramifications.

'I'll see the Director at once, and could you ask the Chief Justice and the Attorney General when they can see me?' Then we'll book prime time. Joss, we'll nip this in the bud.'

'You're angry, Mr President!'

'You're right I'm goddam angry, and this gives me a chance to say something I've been meaning to say for a long time. Ruthlessness and unchecked ambition have ruled too long in the boardroom and, alas, in the department offices of state, and if some guy with a conscience blows the whistle, they're hounded without mercy. The strong have a duty to the weak. The survival of the fittest is for the jungle, not for humanity!'

Joss took his leave at once, his step much lighter.

*

The scene was familiar. The President was behind his Oval Office desk, but this time flanked by the Chief Justice and the Attorney General.

Sarah was watching from behind the cameras when the finger pointed.

'My fellow Americans, you will be aware of the sudden death of the multi-billionaire Glit Jones. He was found beside the shattered fragments of a vase, the priceless favourite of his collection. The doctors are certain that violent shock caused the fatal seizure.

'Few ever saw the Jones mansion home and its collection. His treasure was for him alone. As you no doubt know, Jones started his career as a rock star, made a lot of money and put it into real estate. His fortune mushroomed, but he didn't seek the headlines. He was content to watch his empire grow, and grow it did, as did his art collection. Jones was immensely wealthy. Some have called him an obsessive eccentric. That, of course, is not a crime, indeed, eccentrics can and do enrich our lives. But, you see, that is not the whole story.

'Like the compulsive collector that he was, Jones kept all his deals and transactions in neatly labelled boxes. These have been found to reveal a monstrous web of corruption, which has ensnared half a dozen City Halls. Bribery was his method and blackmail his security. A number of well-known figures are involved and they will face the rigour of the law. Jones always went to the top. Senior members of corporate law firms; boardroom bosses and the most lucrative of them all, senior public servants, those, including mayors, who knew the forward plans for town expansion. Now, if that's not bad enough, Jones also documented the hounding of honest staff that dared to talk. Some were corrupted, and here it's easy for us to condemn, but with children at school, a mortgage, health care and the rest, what would we have done? In some cases we will modify the severity of the law. Indeed, the Presidential pardon may be used.

'My fellow Americans, there will be no cover-up, no back-stairs deals, no stitch-up. Your President is angry that senior public office has been used to feed unchecked ambition. Such behaviour is intolerable. It corrupts the state like dry rot eating at the wooden sinews of a house. I hear too much of boardroom bullies who are held up as examples of so-called thrusting corporate excellence. I'm tired of little town hall Caesars, who treat their office like a private fief. Public service *is* a service and a duty, but corruption is a virulent disease that must be rooted out.

'Recently, I visited some run-down areas in our cities. Now, folks, how can we expect these people to reform, when their city icons feed upon corruption?'

'Corruption will destroy in half an hour what men have taken years of patient work to build. We must not sleep upon our watch. Freedom is earned.'

'Good night, and thank you for your attention.'

Slowly the screen image of the Oval Office faded.

*

Sarah was watching her husband chatting amiably to the Chief Justice, when she saw the Attorney General Jim Burrows approach. She had met him on a number of occasions. A rotund man, rather like her picture of a friendly bank manager.

'That was powerful, ma-am. What was your impression?'

'The strange case of the shattered vase! Sounded like an Agatha Christie!'

'You've put your finger right on it, for without the shattered vase, the whole frightening web would still be thriving.'

'Do you think there's more out there?'

'Yes, but nothing as grotesque as this: I hope tonight will encourage honest men to speak up.'

'Brave men!'

'Yes, when rent-a-thug is round the corner. We'll emphasize the confidential line, of course, but then you get the cranks. Things are never quite straightforward. Ah, here's Joss.'

'Joss, you look as though you've shed a burden.'

'I have. This morning I was despondent, but he's turned it round, completely round.'

'Not completely; there'll be some overheated politician trying to make some capital.'

'Jim, you don't have to tell me. And there'll be some tabloid editor trying to boost his figures. I can see the headline, "Duncan acts quickly to save his political skin." Why do they write such hogwash?'

'They would, wouldn't they?' Sarah quipped, recalling the famous one-liner.

*

It was Ed Vince, Whitehead's energetic staffer, that proved Jim Burrows' point, as the Senator and he were entering their temporary campaign office the following morning.

One of the habitual posse of waiting reporters called out louder than his colleagues.

'Ed, what did you think of the President last evening.'

'Anything for political capital! There wasn't need for such a goddam fuss. We have an FBI. OK?'

'Hey, fellas', the Senator interviened immediately. 'Ed's been working long and sleeping short. I agree with the President. This scandal shouldn't be a political football. That's it. OK?'

Then they passed inside. Whitehead was furious.

'Ed, think before you speak! Duncan meant every word he said last night. Don't attack an honest man, it's dangerous! OK? So you leave it to the FBI and every paper's howling that the President is indifferent and then it *is* political. Haven't you read the morning's papers? They're all behind him, except for one or two that do more harm than good. Jeez, Ed, wise up!'

Ed didn't like it but he held his tongue. He'd never seen the Senator so riled.

Chapter Forty-One

Sarah had never been to Chicago, except in transit via O'Hare International. O'Hare was in a sense the central hub, the airport from which a myriad of connecting flights proceeded, and it was claimed to be the busiest in the world. Not in her wildest dreams had she imagined that her second visit would be in Air Force One; certainly not as the First Lady! No cramped, cattle-truck conditions here, she thought wryly. This time, of course, she would actually be visiting the Windy City, nestling, as it did, at the southern end of Lake Michigan.

The Democratic Convention was again a first. For a prominent media person it was an odd omission, but that was how it was. The venue with its non-stop razzmatazz hadn't attracted her. This time, though, there was no option. It was her duty.

John said little on the flight. The polls still tipped in Whitehead's favour and so much hung on this one single occasion. It was make or break, Billy Benson kept repeating with insensitive regularity. John, though, didn't seem to mind. Joss, of course, was already at the Convention, pumping hands and reassuring all that John would pull it off.

To her English mind Chicago was synonymous with Al Capone and all the old-style gangster myth. There was a legendary Democratic boss called Daly. She'd remembered the clip of him and JFK meeting at the time of the Cuban crisis, which reinforced her feeling of a hard-nosed wheeler-dealer undercurrent. John only laughed when she told him.

Joss didn't dislike the politicking, but a day on the floor of the convention took its toll. It was a chance to meet many old friends and acquaintances. But there was a tension in the atmosphere. Lagging in the polls was not the food of optimism. It was hard work, especially as he himself was full of doubts.

'If only he'd take a swipe at Whitehead. He needs to get out there, Joss. The Mr Nice Guy stuff ain't working!' This was the common theme.

'He'll pull it off. He always does. Keep the faith,' Joss kept repeating. What else could he say?

*

It was all predictable: the prepared speech abandoned, the teleprompt taken away, and Duncan standing alone and silent after the thunder of the initial reception. The moment had arrived.

'My fellow Americans, it is a privilege to address our Democratic assembly, which is part of the great two-party system that guards our Constitution. We hold democracy dear. Indeed, it is a wonderful safety valve for conflicting social pressures. But without the presence of a will to nurture excellence, without that and the guardianship of justice, democracy, with votes the prize, merely panders to the greatest number, while the minority being of the lesser number, withers. So, if this reasoning be correct, and without intending any personal or culinary offence, democracy in its crudest form simply gives the overfed more food!'

Sarah, sitting close behind, willed him to change direction. It was a powerful beginning but he needed something light. He needed laughter. Then, as if he'd heard her thoughts, he stopped, smiling widely; it was like throwing a switch.

'Hey, I've had a great year. I went for a walk-in-the-park.' He chuckled. 'Some thought the colloquial meaning was appropriate! But I wasn't crazy; I saw the people face-to-face without the usual ring of bodyguards. Somehow I rediscovered humanity and simple decency. There it was before my eyes. I sensed a natural harmony in which all of us were held and all we had to do was tune ourselves to it.

'Don't worry, I hadn't gone to fairyland. No, this is practical stuff and the questions that I've bored you with are part of that. Do you remember them, though?'

'What is' – he prompted.

'Location value,' they finished in a bellowed confusion.

'Not much of a choir,' he said, pretending disappointment. 'I'll conduct you.'

This was slapstick, Sarah thought, but it was good crowd participation and it hammered home the message.

'Yeah, I've had a great year,' he continued, after the clamour had receded. 'I got married. Now, how did a shop-soiled guy like me get so lucky?'

Instant pandemonium erupted; this was the chance for high spirits to let off steam, for bugles and for trumpets and all the sundry music makers. After five minutes or so, the noise level dropped.

'I take it you approve. It's just as well, for if you hadn't, I'd have called the Joint Chiefs!'

A spontaneous roar of laughter followed and Duncan flashed a happy smile at Sarah. Then for some moments the President stood quite still, waiting for the hall to come to silence.

'By now, you will have concluded that location value is community created and by reason belongs to its creator. Of course, real estate law is long established but it condones the private confiscation of the public fund. It divides the have-nots from the haves: those on one side of the track and those on the other. Now I've pushed the boat out! Tomorrow I'll be savaged in the press and yet again the White House Press Officer Billy Benson will be having kittens. The place is already teeming with the creatures! But don't panic; don't be rushing to the barricades. As my old friend Seb Sebbson keeps repeating, move the compass slowly.

'Collecting the community value is not a tax. It's a duty due. But to collect anything like the total duty overnight would be madness. Change would be gradual. There'd be no instant paupers; such harsh measures are simply inhumane. Indeed, what we propose is a gradual shift in revenue collection. Today we take what the individual creates and leave what the community creates. We propose the opposite, leave what belongs to the individual – his earnings and take what belongs to the community – the location value. Presently we fund infrastructure out of general taxation. Such improvements boost location value, which benefits private and corporate real estate interests. So you might say that the poor, by virtue of the tax they pay, help the rich get richer. Whereas if location value were collected by the community, the revenue would fund the infrastructure and in turn further boost location value, which is, of course, the community's fund.

'Folks, this is exciting stuff. To tap the laws lying patiently in nature is no mean thing. But many will react, and fiercely; *this* unworkable proposal, they'll complain; *this* out-of-date theory; *this* dreamland of naivety. They are wrong. The natural law is working *now*. It cannot be ignored. If we obey, we have one result; if we don't, another. There's no point blaming the creator for our disobedience. We have the choice. It's our decision! The history boys tell us that economic fortunes run in cycles and to claim that we control these is rather like your President claiming he controls the tides. Yet if we trim our sails to nature's laws these cycles are not dire; if we don't, of course, extreme reactions are the end result. This isn't only about accountancy or simply bottom line. It's a moral issue where right and wrong are seen in high relief. We may not like this if we're sitting pretty. We may feel outraged. Indeed, we may go dutifully to church on Sunday, but, you know, there're seven days in every week. Let's replace the economics of the madhouse with an economic system based on justice, and by so doing free this land for enterprise. It won't be easy. If it were it would simply be the same old thing repackaged. You can have the Glit Jones of this world amassing grotesque wealth in real estate, while others spend their weekly earnings on an attic; in fact, the same old thing.

'What a citizen earns by honest work is their affair, and, as long as that citizen pays the due location value, on, say, a monthly or an annual basis, the land that he requires is also his affair. I've said more than I meant to say, much more. Should I have kept silent on these issues? Should I have said what vested interest wants to hear? Should I forget the curse of inner city squalor? Should I forget about the unemployed, or unemployable as most would have us think? Hope makes men and women employable. Indeed, my wish would be that all, who had the will, could set up for themselves. But it seems that everything conspires against it, for tax and regulation are like vultures waiting for a fresh and tasty meal. Then there's the landlord. He's there, no matter how run-down the shack is that we want to hire. The shack may be worth nothing, of course, but the *location* is! We need to free up excess. Let the landlord pay his location value duty. Then let him charge a rental for his building only. Then let the game begin, and, as I've just said, let's free this land for enterprise!'

Changing course again, Duncan turned to world affairs. His mastery was obvious. How did he do it? Sarah wondered: such a kaleidoscope of detail.

'It is always easy to criticize, and, as you know, America doesn't suffer from a lack of that. But, my friends, her President doesn't have a crystal ball. He can only act on what he sees to be the best advice, and at times decision hangs by very slender threads. He should be slow to move, yet instant when the need occurs. Criminals we can deal with; mostly they possess some common sense. Fanatics, though, are dangerous, for they can crash the world about our ears because of some delusion. Vigilance is imperative.'

The President continued with his survey, but Joss was very much distracted. This wasn't a conference speech, a rallying of the troops. The world scene was OK, but location value was a vote killer. Every garden suburb would be hard against it! The hosts of heaven couldn't win against such vested interest; and no mention of the shortfalls in Republican policy – nothing! Joss was despondent.

As if on cue, Duncan's speech turned to focus on this very party subject.

'You will have noticed that I haven't had a swipe at Sam Whitehead. The reason is simple. I admire the Senator and I'm certainly not going to attack him for the sake of it. Of course, the election game will proceed, but I for one will refrain from any character attack. That, of course, does not preclude a healthy and vigorous debate on issues. My fellow Americans, what we are about is much too important to be diverted by trivialities. Truth initially may be unpopular, but when the harvest comes, it's rich and lasting.

'We're going for the bundle. This is not the time to hide behind banalities; the patchwork promises that seduce, but only for an hour! We must free the citizen from the burden of trapped hopelessness. Gather to the state her rightful fund, and, once the trend is set in motion, we must not let it be reversed. My friends, the natural order *is* our rightful constitution.'

The President paused and pulled a diary-sized book out of his inside pocket. The hall was completely silent, the delegates fascinated. He held the book aloft.

'Some months ago I quoted from this book; you may have watched. It's called *Gems from Henry George*. The experts tell me George is past his sell-by date. Well, do you know something – I think I'll stick with George! Listen to this.

I believe that any great social improvement must spring from, and be animated by, that spirit which seeks to make life better, nobler and happier for others, rather than the spirit which only seeks more enjoyment for itself. For the Mammon of Injustice can always buy the selfish whenever it may think it worth while to pay enough; but unselfishness it cannot buy.'

'That's it, folks, and may the spirit that animated this great

American, Henry George, inspire us all.'

The Hall was completely silent as the President casually waved and left the platform. Billy Benson was sitting bent forward, his head in his hands. Joss sat drained of energy. John had lost it, thrown it away, but Harry Roberts felt that something strange had happened, something special. Sarah was weeping; she could only see the President. The silence held. Then, as if responding to some hidden signal, the Conference Hall erupted.

Billy Benson looked up amazed at what he saw. Jeez, they're going mad, he whispered. He turned to Joss. Both were on their feet.

'He's done it!' Joss bellowed. 'But only God knows how.'

Harry Roberts, too, was on his feet. The feeling that he'd had had been confirmed. He watched as the President took Sarah by the hand and led her to the platform. He turned to Mary at his side; she was wide-eyed and in shock. He squeezed her hand and then her tears began to flow.

*

'Senator Whitehead, his cousin Hal, Ed Vince and Joe Smolensky were huddled round the wide-screen TV in their campaign quarters. Empty beer cans littered the glass-topped coffee table.

Raising himself from his battered armchair, Ed hurried over to the fridge and grabbed another can.

'Duncan's thrown it away. All this sentimental hogwash *don't* bring in the votes. He's out to lunch. He's lost it. Over the hill - you name it.'

'What do you think, Hal?' the Senator interjected.

'Everything he said was true. I couldn't fault him.'

'Hal, he's fingered real estate. Tell me where they haven't got both hands on that?' Ed interjected.

'The inner city rat holes.'

'Who cares? They don't vote!'

'What do you think, Joe?' the Senator asked.

'Duncan's not a wimp, but Ed is right: most only think about the bottom line. Their vision doesn't stretch beyond the garden fence. And what do you think, Senator?'

'They were going wild in that hall today and the media fellas weren't much better. Maybe he's shown them the vision that's beyond the fence!'

'Yeah,' Ed said cynically.

'Ed, don't attack Duncan. I mean it. OK.'

'Jeez, Senator, he's set himself up!' Vince shook his head, his frustration obvious.

Chapter Forty-Two

Now at the hotel suite, the President sat back in his easy chair and kicked his shoes off. He yawned.

'John, you ought to have a rest.'

'That's wishful thinking, the phone...'

'I'll tell them no more calls for half an hour.'

'Simple. Would that such economy of action ruled the world!'

'John, what happened today?'

'I'm as puzzled as you are, my love. I just focused on the essence and out it came. It was way under the radar! Mind you, there was a cautious fella snapping at my heels, but he was bloodless.'

'John, I've witnessed many speeches. It was my job. There was more to it than that.'

'I don't know, Sarah, maybe something found its perfect pitch. Perhaps I stumbled into nature's symphony – a kind of accidental hacker!'

'Wonderful imagery! I think you've got it!'

'It's poetry, Sarah; but there's one thing I'm sure of. There was a lot of space out there.'

'Don't knock poetry, John. It's a subtle language.'

'I know, my love, but the coalface is the coalface. There ain't much poetry there!'

'There was today!'

Duncan laughed.

'Time to rest, Mr President; you've got the reception this evening!'

'Yes, ma-am,' he replied, saluting formally.

*

The buffet reception, in some ways, was a chaos of endless brief and hearty greetings. However, it was clear that many were unsettled. His speech had challenged limits and, of course, self-interest, the latter rising like an evening mist. Time and time again he reassured the party faithful.

'This isn't a Maoist revolution, fellas. It's just a shift to funding in a natural way and in the end we'd all be better off. Listen, we're not a communion of saints, so a hundred per cent collection is way, way off the screen. Ask Seb; he'll fill you in. As he says, he's just as hard-nosed as any of us.'

Thus the evening proceeded. There was no outright rebellion, but it was clear to Duncan that an acceptance of this natural reform would take some time and patience.

*

Afterwards Joss, Harry, Seb, and Jake Crystal gathered in the President's suite.

'We all earned our keep this evening, guys,' the President quipped. 'Thank God I stuck to mineral water. Now I can have a decent glass of red!'

'That I second,' Seb said instantly.

'Well, what do you think? Have we pushed the boat too far?' The President continued. 'What do you think, Harry?'

'I'm basing my faith on your Convention speech. That sound reached the stars, and that only happens when the time is ripe. As you keep saying, Seb, you probably have a patent on it, move the compass slowly, but we gotta move, we can't stand still!'

'Well folks,' the President responded, 'that being the case, we have a lot to do from now until November. So Joss, I propose you court the party bosses. And Joss, I'll join you now and then, but in the meantime, though, I'll take another inner city tour. Harry, you can come with me and when you're not with me, you can keep Joss on the straight and narrow! Seb and Jake, you're already doing a great job – but no public platform stuff. OK! Where's Billy?'

'Out trying to get the first editions,' Harry answered.

'That's Billy, *and* he'll get them. Did anyone see the chat shows?'

'Tom Goodwin, Billy's assistant,' Joss replied. 'He's next floor down.'

'Let's bring him in.'

Joss immediately lifted the phone.

Tom Goodwin had a tall, languid figure. Duncan thought of him as a latter-day Jimmy Stewart, but there was nothing languid about his mind. Tom was sharp. A knock heralded his arrival.

'Thanks, Tom. Sorry to drag you here so late, but I'm told you watched the chat shows.'

'Yes, Mr President, I felt they hadn't figured out a line.'

'Your meaning, Tom?'

'Well, Sir, it seemed they hadn't really absorbed your message. These guys usually discuss personalities and current opinion but not principles. I'm not saying they're stupid. It's just that it's new territory. They were cautious, Sir.'

'Interesting, Tom. We've been imbibing. Now I don't want to lead you astray, but would you like a nightcap?'

'Sir, I'm already well outside the track!'

Duncan was amused; he liked Tom.

There was a bustling sound in the anteroom and suddenly Billy Benson was amongst them.

'They're all leading on the pandemonium thing after the speech. But hardly a goddam word about the actual speech itself.'

'It's the same as the media boys, Billy,' Joss grumbled.

'I think you've got something to say, Tom,' the President prompted.

'Well, Mr President, I feel the media world tend to see any motive other than self-interest as incredible.'

'You could be right, Tom, but what an arid world. I suppose it's too early for Leo Pucci and Ed Morrison.'

'Yes, Sir,' Billy returned. 'Articles usually take another day.'

'If they print them,' Jake spoke up. He usually was the silent one.

'Meaning, Jake?' Duncan prompted.

'The Editor may have reservations, but I don't feel that will be the problem. It's the proprietors. They won't like the President's words on real estate.' Jake, let a smile escape. 'Well, if they refuse to print, *I will!* Ed and Leo won't be unemployed!'

'I like it, Jake. Listen, guys, the ladies are looking our way. It's midnight and tomorrow is another day.'

As they were leaving, the President beckoned Billy Benson.

'Billy, bring Tom Goodwin with you in the bird tomorrow.'

'Yes, Mr President.'

Air Force One was in the air, the seat belt signs were off and the President was in conference with Joss. Billy Benson and Tom Goodwin were buried in the morning papers and Harry was surfing the breakfast news bulletins. In another corner Sarah,

Joan Johnson and Mary Roberts were discussing charity work, where the First Lady had been asked to act as patron. With her English background she needed guidance to negotiate the local nuances.

'Joss, tell Tom Goodwin all you know', the President was saying. 'Let him see you chatting up the party patriarchs. You're a born diplomat, Joss. Give him a master class.'

'What will I tell Billy?'

'That Tom has been seconded as your PA. Billy's got researchers that he can call on. They're all panting for the next rung on the ladder. Joss, I like Tom; I can work with him. I just would like to see him filled out a little.'

Joss said nothing. The President was hatching something: something long-term. That meant his friend John Duncan hadn't given up. Hope still burned.

Chapter Forty-Three

Joe Burns looked wizened and pugnacious, but this belied a calm unruffled nature, and, surprisingly, for a small man, he had a deep arresting voice. The President trusted him and he received an almost automatic invitation when Duncan was on tour. The tour began two weeks after the Republican Convention in Florida when Sam Whitehead was confirmed as Candidate. This was simply a formality, but the VP choice took most folk by surprise, though not the White House. Joe Smolensky had achieved his goal, neither by fund donation nor by pressure, but by patient work.

Burns and Roberts struck up a natural rapport right from the beginning, but the big man and the wiry newsman were a contrasting duo. It certainly amused the President, though he kept that to himself. Both men were very well aware of the potential dangers attending the President's sudden appearances. These hellholes, as Joe described them, were volatile, but the President was insistent, indeed almost myopic in his single-minded determination.

'These guys won't vote!' Joe grunted dismissively, when they made the morning's first unscheduled stop. Then the slouching bunch of late teen, early twenties, young men swaggered up. The leader was fingering a knife. It was blatant posturing.

'Man, who's the big cat?'

'The President!'

'Don't mess with me, man. OK?'

'OK, but he's still the President.'

'Ah told ya, man,' the leader waved his knife as if it were a pointer. Then he froze. 'Son of a bitch, Jeez, man, it is the goddam President!'

'Put that knife away!' Harry barked. 'These guys are Secret Service!' he added, nodding to the side. 'They'll cut you up!'

'Yeah, yeah!' the leader sneered, but he put the knife away. 'What's he here for?'

'To talk. Now's your chance!'

'Crap, man, he won't talk to us!'

At that the President approached, and the leader stood as if he were a rabbit in the lights, his belligerence suddenly forgotten.

'Hi,' the President said lightly.

No one answered.

'Say, I ask you what you really want. What would be the first thing you would go for?'

'Respect, man,' the leader didn't hesitate.

'And the second?'

'Hey, man, you're working me too hard!'

Duncan burst out laughing. 'I like it, but you haven't answered.'

'Jobs, man, not some supermarket crap. Real jobs, man!'

'OK. This is the deal. I'll do what I can about the jobs, but you must register to vote, and when the time comes, *vote*, OK?'

'For you, man?'

'Who you vote for is *your* decision, but vote!'

'You got it, Mr President.'

'Let's shake, OK?'

The handshake was elaborate. Duncan guessed it was some gangland ritual.

The crumbling tenement backdrop was a perfect photo opportunity and Joe Burns wasn't idle. This was the President at the coalface, but it was high-risk game. Yet Duncan didn't seem the least perturbed. Now he was talking to a group of women. Some were clutching babies close, while the Secret Service hovered like optimistic vultures. Joe could see that Harry was still in conversation with the teen gang leader. Then suddenly there was the elaborate routine of the handshake.

Brisk and businesslike, the Presidential party left.

'Are we getting through, Harry?' The President asked when they had settled in the limo.

'That was the best one yet, Sir. That gang leader fella was sharp. And you know, these guys have mobiles. Word spreads fast.'

'You had a long chat with Buzz, as he calls himself,' Duncan prompted.

'I hammered on about registering, and exhorted him and all his friends to vote.'

'Will they?'

'Hard to say. Buzz will, but does he have the 'cred' to get the others moving?'

Duncan smiled.

'Bit like me. Do I have the 'cred' to push the Hill towards this natural funding policy?'

'Capitol Hill won't be easy, Sir. We need to try and keep this non-partisan. In fact, we need a substantial Republican ally. Do you know what I'm thinking? No, it's too incredible!'

'Sam Whitehead, I thought of him as well. November, November! It all depends on November! Let's hope the gods are smiling.'

'Yes, Mr President, but we'll need to give them all the help we can!'

They sat silently in the cocoon of the limo as it sped towards the airport and Air Force One.

'What's next, Sir?'

'The local party boss is seeing us off at the airport. He's running hard for mayor, so there'll be more photo opportunities.'

'And after that, Sir?

'Well, as you know, we have no scheduled plan. We've been to Atlanta, Memphis and to New Orleans and I'm tempted to return to Washington, but Houston and the West Coast beckons. We need a spread and, where we can, we need to meet the party faithful. We'll decide the next stop when we're aloft. Have *you* any suggestions, Harry?'

'We're doing fine, Sir. It's like waiting for the call!'

The President laughed.

'You got it.'

*

Ed Vince was irrepressible. They were out in front and looking good. Indeed he had no doubt at all that it was in the bag. In fact, it was almost too easy, for Duncan seemed to have a death wish.

'Imagine', he exulted, 'Duncan's touring slums and telling them to register. He's nuts. They're dropouts, for crissake. All they want is drugs and welfare!'

Sam Whitehead said nothing. Part of him was keen to cheer Ed on, but the greater part was cautious. Duncan wasn't nuts, but he was going full tilt for his policy, for all he said was to that end. Whitehead had watched his Convention speech three times. In one sense it was political suicide, yet its honesty shone out and was no doubt why the delegates had gone crazy. Whitehead couldn't fault John Duncan. Indeed, he felt like some fated medieval jouster commanded by the King to fight the man he most admired. Yet, riding tandem, as it were, ambition still desired the White House.

Whitehead smiled. If Ed only sensed a whiff of this, he surely would invent new swearwords yet unknown.

Chapter Forty-Four

Most thought it but few said it: that the President had thrown away his second term on his obsession. It was now two days to the election and the polls hadn't shifted. Indeed, if anything, the President had lost more ground. He, not the Democrats, had been singled out and the onslaught in the press had been relentless. The vested interest had fought back with unforgiving vigour. No one, if they possessed the smallest modicum of sense, would dare to touch the right to real estate again. Community created value could be claimed as private property, and earnings, the private property of the individual could be taxed. According to the polls, democracy was about to speak. The *status quo* had won.

Joss never for a moment breathed I-told-you-so, though Billy Benson was much less diplomatic. Against the trend Tom Goodwin still held out. This wasn't a-run-of-the-mill election, he maintained. Pollsters weren't infallible and some new, yet crucial sampling, not significant in the past, could well have been ignored. Harry Roberts supported him. To Harry, everything was in place. The work had been done, the people prepared, and an understanding President was in place. Yet, if it were the truth before its time, then that was it. No matter, they had done what could be done and certainly the President had not been idle. In the traditional sense, they had fought the fight.

John Duncan simply waited, so much so that Sarah marvelled at his stoicism.

'It's not stoicism, my love, I'm simply waiting and there hasn't been that inner feeling that the day is lost. Mind you, it may come, but so far it's been strangely absent, for Billy tells me daily, with his usual "diplomatic" bluntness, just how bad things are!'

Sarah laughed.

'Well, John, I'll wait too, but I may be jumpy now and then!'

On the morning of the election Harry went to Dupont Circle and had a coffee at a café that he knew. The customers were the usual mix of solitaries buried in the morning's paper; women having tête-à-têtes; one young man was busy with his laptop. Two eager business types were leafing through a catalogue: a salesman and his client maybe. At times their speech was audible.

'I never vote,' one said dismissively. 'Those fellas are out for themselves. But I tell you something. I'm going to the polling booth this time.'

'Jeez, Ed, that's exactly how I feel. This guy tells it straight.'

Almost at once they turned their heads away, busy with the catalogue again. Were they Duncan men? Harry felt they were. It fitted. Certainly the President had told it straight, *too* straight for many!

Harry slipped out. No one had recognized him, or so it seemed. At Dupont station he took the metro to Washington Center, where he changed and headed for the Smithsonian. Emerging from the metro, he began to walk towards the Washington Monument with its usual clutch of tourists. There was a general sense of calm about the city and he didn't think that his perception was imagination.

Then he headed for the Lincoln Memorial, to where, one might say, it had all begun: the morning of the President's 'disappearance.' Harry chose a bench where he could watch the visitors climb the steps to Lincoln's seated statue. Once more he felt the overriding sense of calm. The nation was deciding, the mood reflective. Yes, he thought instinctively, it was going to the wire.

In anticipation of sleepless hours ahead, the President and Sarah had planned to rest in the afternoon and early evening. It would be a long night, especially if the race were close. The polls, of course, continued to predict a Whitehead win and Billy Benson said the Democratic rooms were like an Irish Wake. Then, Billy would say that!

Just after polling closed, Joss and Harry returned to the White House, having completed a quick tour of polling stations both in DC and in Maryland. The common message from the sites had been the same: a heavy poll and a late surge that was thought to favour Duncan. It was, as Harry felt all afternoon, going to the wire.

Sam Whitehead was in Kansas City, where a sudden chill had dulled the well-established mood of optimism. The exit polls were showing worrying trends and the turn-out was unusually high. This mostly favoured the Democrats. Ed Vince and Joe Smolensky were still upbeat, but the Senator was uncertain, though he kept that to himself. Duncan had focused on the areas of inner-city deprivation. Whitehead's thoughts were sobering. He had listened to his strategists, who'd been adamant that such canvassing was a total waste of time. Naturally, Duncan's various forays had been reported. Indeed, one or two of the more entertaining episodes had been repeated *ad nauseam* on the news programmes and this may have captured the idealistic impulses of the young. He should have overruled these experts, but now it was too late.

Thwarted by a continuous stream of phone calls, the President gave up all attempts at resting. In the afternoon the calls had been little other than veiled commiseration. Then with the exit polls the tone had changed dramatically. Indeed, some party grandees, who had studiously distanced themselves, were suddenly back on stream. Even so, Duncan was cautious. Nothing was certain until the line was crossed and that was some way off. In fact, they didn't even have the first result.

Bursts of elation came and went, but Duncan's predominant feeling was that of being an onlooker. It was happening to someone else! People now were praising the boldness of his strategy, but the truth was that he'd had no strategy as such. Indeed, if he *had* proposed the strategy most people were assuming, he'd have been labelled crazy. He had simply followed his instinct and his inner promptings. Slum poverty was unacceptable and by his actions he'd hoped to give example. It was time democracy catered for all and not only for the greatest number. It was time to stop, instead of slipping by on the other side. Handouts were the usual social democratic answer, but they were temporary, and it bred dependence. Respect, as Buzz had answered, held the key and justice sprang the lock, beyond which the simple laws of nature waited.

An energetic knock heralded another visit from Billy Benson.

'It's looking good, Sir, and if the exit polls are right we've moved ahead!'

'Billy, what about the Irish Wake?'

'The late lamented got up for a whiskey, Sir!'

Duncan burst out laughing.

Chapter Forty-Five

The night was relentless and in the early stages it was neck and neck. Predictions were impossible and the commentators cautious; indeed, they hadn't any explanation for the Duncan surge. Then New York and Pennsylvania declared for Duncan, but Florida went Republican. After that New Jersey voted Duncan, and so the night went on until it was obvious that California, in the end, would hold the key. If Duncan received their fifty-five electoral votes he'd have a clear majority but if Whitehead won, his mandate would be slender. It was going to the wire, as Harry had predicted.

Excusing himself, the President shuffled off to bed and most followed his example. Only Joss, Billy Benson and Tom Goodwin kept vigil, although they dozed from time to time and for substantial periods.

Morning came with interest in the Californian result at fever pitch. Commentators were still pouring out words. Exit polls were conflicting, but those in the major cities were showing a Duncan bias. Harry, who had just joined the weary vigil, felt his prediction to be cruelly true. It was to the wire with a vengeance. Thankfully, the President had spent a considerable time on the West Coast. Had his efforts born fruit? That was the question.

It took two more hours before the answer came. The President had topped the poll and this time it was substantial. John Duncan had been returned for four more years.

Then, as expected, came the traditional phone call from Sam Whitehead, conceding victory to the President. The words of both men were generous. In fact, one newspaper printed the photographs of both men on its front page, with the heading, 'Two Honourable Men'. It was a pity, the leader ran, that one had to lose. 'Sentimental hogwash,' one media icon reacted, a view shared by many of his colleagues. Both men, they echoed, had simply made the same PR calculation. This, in turn, was ridiculed by Leo Pucci in a humorous skit, entitled, 'Be one of us, be cynical.'

*

For weeks Sarah had been certain that her sojourn in the White House would end in January. John's tour of the inner city slums had been commendable but hardly practical, from the point of view of garnering votes, a view tutored by her media years. The desire to speak had been frequent, but the need to speak, she had discerned, was absent. John had been well aware of the general mood of discontent - Billy Benson made sure of that! – and she'd had no wish to add her voice to that. Thank God she'd held her tongue. Joss, loyal to the end, had bit his lip, but Harry had been right behind the President. He shared the principles that John held close and dear. She had played the disc of John's convention speech a number of times and, with John's help, even she could see the amazing potential of the measure he proposed. It was strangely emotional, she'd confided and John had smiled. 'That's it; you've got it. Now we're even more a team!'

*

In the first week of December Harry Roberts escorted Sam Whitehead to the Oval Office. He had been invited to a private lunch in the Presidential quarters and Harry was the only other guest.

Both President and Senator greeted each other warmly and after some preliminary pleasantries they went upstairs.

'Lunch in your private quarters I take to be a signal honour, Mr President.'

'Sam, when you've heard my "grand design" you may have second thoughts! Now to serious matters: what's your poison?' Duncan asked, opening the drinks cupboard.

'A small glass of white is my lunchtime measure.'

'Harry?'

'The same, Sir.'

'Let's all be measured,' the President returned; then he carefully poured three glasses and handed them round. 'Sarah is out with Joan Johnson, so Jilly, my long-suffering cook, is doing the honours, so we'll await her call.'

Whitehead raised his glass.

'To a fruitful second term, Mr President.'

'And to you, Senator, a career worthy of your powers.'

'Can I ask a question, Sir?'

Duncan nodded.

'What was the secret of your surge? The answers I've been given are Machiavellian to the point of absurdity!'

'Sam, it surprised us too! We can't ascribe it to the semi no-go areas of the inner cities. That would be naïve. But I believe Harry put his finger on it.' Duncan nodded in Harry's direction. 'Your shot.'

'On election morning I went to Dupont Circle and had a coffee in a bar I know; testing the mood, as it were. There were two young bloods leafing through a catalogue and I overheard a snatch of conversation. It was something like this: "I never vote, but I'm voting this time. This guy tells it straight." Now, my theory is that the three questions, the Convention speech, which was politically neutral, and the shots of the inner city confrontations, especially featuring Buzz, all made an impression on the young. Here was something that they understood. The President was stressing the moral angle and it touched the heart. That's the theory.'

'It figures,' Whitehead responded. 'For my part, I agreed with everything the President was saying; and being vaguely honest, there was no target that I felt I could attack!'

'Sam,' the President interjected. 'Your honesty is made of sterner stuff. It was a rock, and that is why you're here! Ah, I hear Jilly. Lunch is served.'

Sam Whithead was careful to acknowledge Jilly, and compliment the artistry of her starter. Jilly beamed, as did the President. For him another box was ticked.

After he had sampled the starter, Whitehead looked up.

'Mr President, you're keeping me hanging out there. You were about to tell me something.'

'Sam,' Duncan began, 'these principles I've been hammering on about are self-evident. They shouldn't be a political football. Indeed, what I'm saying is, we should make this bi-partisan. It may be pie in the sky, but we should, at least, try.'

'A true principle shouldn't be a party battering ram or target, but I fear the party boys will rush to gather to themselves the vested interest opposition. It's tailor made!'

'Senator, it won't be easy, but then that which is worthwhile rarely is. As Harry here would say, the gods have given us the opportunity. Much of the jigsaw is in place. It would be wrong to wallow in a sea of doubt. At least we can lead the horse to the water!'

'What about timing, Sir?'

'To ask you to move immediately would be grossly insensitive. Things need to settle. Easter, maybe, there'll be a time. In the meanwhile you and Harry might jaw a little and maybe earmark men of calibre. It's early days. But Sam, you may feel that this would wreck your chances of a shot in four years' time. Don't mind Duncan. Do what your inner self dictates.'

'If I did run, and it is an if, there's nothing to stop me running on the ticket we're discussing; indeed, knowing what I know, what other ticket could I run on? But I'd have a tough fight in the primaries, for the vested interest would be bound to field a candidate.'

'I guess they would,' the President said quietly.

Chapter Forty-Six

Projects, enquiries and staffing questions suspended during the run-up to the election were now alive and pressing. Joss was inundated, and on top of that the President wanted to see him at twelve thirty, which was, of course, the lunchtime slot. Tom Goodwin was helping, but he was visiting his ailing father. Indeed, everything seemed to be conspiring to make his working day impossible.

He looked at the clock. It was almost time, so getting to his feet he made his way to the Oval Office and knocked gently. The President was behind his desk, but got up immediately and headed for the sofa. It was the sign of informality.

'Joss, how long have you been keeping me on the straight and narrow?'

'I've been trying for fifteen years!'

Duncan laughed briefly.

'Yes, the Senate was the toughest test, and without you I never would have made it. You know, you've always been there and these last few months must have been purgatory, for I've been playing maverick.

'Four more years now lie ahead of us, and Joss, I feel you need a change. Chief of Staff is a wearing job and you're always in the shadow of the President.'

Joss said nothing. Clearly the President wanted a new and younger man.

'Well, Joss, this is it! The CIA Director is retiring. Would you like the job?'

Joss again said nothing. Shock had followed shock.

'Joss, are you there?'

'Mr President, is this OK? I have no experience in that field.'

'You're a man of total integrity. You don't leave stuff lying in your pending tray. And no one will pull the wool over your eyes! And if you don't like the job Andy Anderson doesn't want to serve the full four years.'

'Secretary of State, I don't have the experience! And Congress will have to confirm...'

'Don't worry Joss, they'll find no skeletons. As I've said before, you're too damned dull! And, Joss, the CIA posting will raise your profile. Remember you did study International Affairs at college and you got a top mark.'

'That's a long time ago.'

'It may be, but you've always had an interest in the international scene. Joss you're a born diplomat. You've met most of the world leaders. I made sure of that. Joss, I didn't think this up yesterday. Anyway, this CIA role will ease you into prominence. Now, I'm not downgrading the CIA directorship, for it's a major posting.'

Joss sat, bewildered by his sudden change of circumstances.

'Yes, I agree the CIA job isn't just a stepping-stone. It's a humbling responsibility!'

'Now you know how *I* feel!'

'Yes,' the sound was drawn out and almost a whisper.

'Let's go upstairs; Sarah has prepared something. What about Tom, could he fill your shoes?' the President added as they left the room.

'Yes, he has a cool head. He's young, but he'll soon age!'

Duncan chuckled.

'Now, Joss, here's another, the VP slot, our old friend Zac is losing his vigour. He wants to go, he grumbles, but as you know he bounces back. He's as tough as they come. But whom should I nominate as his successor? We don't need to rush. In fact, something tells me not to hurry. Yet I'm uneasy, for whoever I nominate I make a natural front runner for the next election and how can I put forward someone ignorant of the principles we hold dear?'

Joss Johnson shook his head.

'I've no idea what to say.'

'Think about it; let it circulate a little. I'll tell you what my thoughts are when we've had our lunch.'

Harry closed the door noiselessly, his whole attention focused on the simple act. The President watched, sharing the attention. The big man was still trim and with such a powerful frame he was surprisingly nimble. People were attracted by his unassuming ways and the gentle sense of presence he exuded. Most knew about his service in the Gulf, but few knew the detail and even fewer knew of his liaison function with the British SAS. Harry wasn't a wimp and by heavens he was capable. In fact, everything that was thrown his way he simply did. Fuss was not a word in Harry's dictionary. Duncan had heard him speak publicly once or twice. On both occasions his words were brief and to the point and there'd been no hint of self-publicity.

'Harry,' the President greeted, rising from his Oval Office swivel chair. 'It seems a long time since the limo days, but what a blessing that you took that job, and what a blessing that we had those few brief words, for I knew you knew what I'd experienced. Indeed, you were the only one I felt that I could talk to.'

'It's been quite a year, I owe you much, Mr President.'

'And you deserve much. How did you get on with Sam?'

'He's tapped the essence. The Senator's with us, Sir'

'What if we make him Chairman of the group that you are forming?'

'A Republican Chairman, yes that would balance your well-known advocacy.'

The President sighed. He rarely did and Harry sensed a weariness. It had been a tough four months.

'We have another term. Four more years to battle vested interest might.'

'What did Victor Hugo, say about "an idea whose time has come?"'

'That it was stronger than armies; something in that line,' the President responded. 'Well, one could say the time is ripe, for much is in place; all we need's the will to change. What is right and what is wrong? Is it right for rich men to get richer by claiming what is meant for all? Not the buildings, not men's labour, but location value, that sum created by the collective presence.'

Harry remained silent. One thing was very clear; the President wouldn't let the question drift.

'You'll be hearing shortly that Joss is to be the new Director of the CIA. It will have to be ratified but that's as good as done. In the meantime keep it under your hat.'

'That *is* good news. No one will take Joss for a ride!'

'Harry, you need more prominence. A man like you needs to be recognized and appreciated. Secretary of State Anderson wants men of integrity to tour areas of unrest. We need to be informed, and not caught napping, as it were. Such assignments will give you the prominence you deserve. And, Harry, maybe some day you will try that for size,' the President added, pointing at the swivel chair behind the Oval Office desk. I'm serious, you're a good man, and the nation needs good men. Who knows what the future will bring? Harry, you know the natural law regarding location value. You know it in you heart. It's not just an intellectual thing. So take my hint seriously. Who knows? Who knows? And don't be surprised if I push you into positions of significance.

'You know, that morning of my "disappearance" changed my life. I somehow fell in love with reason. Now, I do the most unreasonable things!'

A dam of tension burst and both men doubled up with laughter.

Epilogue

Christmas at Camp David was a time of rest. Many of the uncertainties were over, and the path was set, a path from which the President would not deviate. All remarked how both Joss and Harry had grown in stature yet neither tarnished this with any colouring of pomposity.

Tom Goodwin's laconic nature soon adapted to the White House pressures. The President liked him, but he noticed, remembering Joss's knowing aside, that Tom's lingering boyishness had gone. It was not surprising; the White House staff were bright and often gifted people; they could be difficult to deal with and they were not without ambition. So Tom's initiation had not been easy.

The Inauguration took place as tradition dictated on the 20th January on the West Front of the Capitol. His address was short, even briefer than that of President Kennedy, whose famous words he invoked in his conclusion.

'*Ask not what your country can do for you – ask what you can do for your country*, are words that have inspired us all. They are the clarion call of unselfishness. These are not the words of a dependence culture, but those of freedom. *Institutional charity and political expedients are no substitute for Justice*. Again these are not my words but the words of a British Labour politician spoken between the two World Wars.*

'Finally, here is Henry George, a great American, whose wisdom has been largely shelved by modern academics. *It is not enough that [The people] should be theoretically equal before the law. They must have liberty to avail themselves of the opportunities and means of life; they must stand on equal terms, with reference to the bounty of nature. Either this, or liberty withdraws her light! ... Unless its foundations be laid in justice, the social structure cannot stand.* **

'Together let us work on this foundation, and may the Good Lord bless our endeavours.'

❋

The State of the Union address was given on the first week in February. It was in the evening. The doors opened and the words 'The President of the United States' were bellowed out in the customary manner, with the President slowly making his way to the rostrum, shaking hands to left and right as he passed. Before him and above the rostrum were Zac the Vice-President and the Speaker. And there was Harry, sitting amongst the small group of Presidential guests.

The standing ovation continued until the President gestured for an end.

Then came the State of the Union message, listing past achievements and future legislative proposals. Next there was the overseas perspective. The detail was considerable. Of course, the assembled Congress knew that there was more to come. It was clearly expected, for the President had *well* prepared the ground throughout the previous year.

'My friends, I need your help. What I propose is simple, yet insensitive application of simplicity can be damaging. But, Members of Congress, we need to *start*. This is no ordinary proposal. We intend shifting the burden of tax from work and enterprise and catch the shortfall with the duty from community-created value that is due to location. All this, you've heard before. Ideally the individual would take what he creates and the community what it creates. It is as simple as that, and for my part self-evident. It is a moral question and a question for us all. We are one nation; this is not a Democratic 'thing' or a Republican 'thing.' We aim to trash this curse of poverty at its roots, not perpetuate it with handouts, and meagre ones at that. When I toured the inner city slums one young man I met impressed me greatly; his name was Buzz; you may have viewed the incident on the box. When I asked what he really wanted, his answer was "Respect." To me, this was the voice of dignity and I heard it in the crumbling slums.

'The creator did not intend the deprivation in our midst. We with our free will and our ignorance of the natural order have created it. We Americans are a generous people. Yet, when confronted with the no-man's-land of poverty, we walk by on the other side. Perhaps, seeing the enormity of the problem, we turn aside in hopeless impotence. How dare we tolerate these drug-infested hellholes! Most of you were present at the Inauguration. You will have heard the words of Henry George. We are proud of our liberty. Indeed, we have built a statue to it. We, as George said, are theoretically equal before the law, but what use is that when we do not stand on equal terms before the ample bounty of nature? Reason demands economic justice, not some sentimental scheme to make us all feel better as we dine in luxury. My friends, I wish no personal offence. We all stand at the bar, including your President. What is proposed is neither a fascist fantasy nor an overbearing socialism but the simple rule of freedom where we are left to find our place in life quite naturally. As I said at the beginning, I need your help. This task is for all of us.'

There was a standing ovation; there always was, of course, but had he done it, had he touched their hearts? He rarely knew, but others told him.

Sarah had been present as a visitor, and when returning in the limo she gave the President his answer.

'John, dear, you did it again.'

'What did I do, my love?'

'They were shining; some were weeping unashamedly!'

'Were they?'

'What were those words you said to Harry?'

'A bit pretentious, I'm afraid; that I'd fallen in love with reason.'

'But, John, that's it. Love and reason, that's what was working tonight!'

'Thank God it wasn't John Duncan!'

She laughed; her captivating laugh was so entrancing.

Happy and smiling, he leaned across and kissed her.

References

* John Stewart, *Standing for Justice*, London, Shepheard-Walwyn 2001 ISBN 0 85683 194 8

** *Gems from Henry George* Originally published in 1912 by A.C.Fifield, London
Republished by the Henry George Foundation of Great Britain in 1930. Reprinted 1931.

T.E. Lawrence – The *Seven Pillars of Wisdom* extract is taken from chapter LXIII p355/356.
Pub. Jonathan Cape London 1935.

VISITORS

John Stewart

'As Einstein observed, "The world cannot get out of the current state of crisis with the same thinking that got it there in the first place". John Stewart, his alien visitors and the people whose lives they touch, know this only too well. Rarely can such a profound message have been delivered in so stimulating and entertaining a fashion.' **Guardian online**

A year into office and the Prime Minister's only bonus was frustration. The swelling demands of welfare and security were like juggernauts, demolishing his reforms and forcing him to spend his time on damage limitation. The economy was overheating, it was said, and interest rates had to the rise. The PM knew the signs and they made him shudder.

Then the Visitors arrived. At first they were treated as illegal immigrants and arrested – the Prime Minister thought the story was a hoax – but when he met these beings from another world, very similar in appearance to humans, he was deeply impressed. They had a presence about them and clearly their civilisation had high technical skills to be able to navigate through space and land on earth.

Meeting the Visitors and asking them questions about how their society was organised, the Prime Minister began to realise here might be some answers to the questions which were currently troubling him and other governments.

'It is difficult to know where to look for comparisons: Graham Greene, for its exquisite prose, or [Arthur C. Clarke], for its deftly imagined other-world politics, and alien beings as thinly disguised representatives of what humankind might one day aspire to.' **Guardian online**

292pp **ISBN 978-0-85683-253-6** **£9.95 pb**

THE LAST ROMANS

A HISTORICAL NOVEL

John Stewart

The story is set in the years following the collapse of Rome at the end of the fifth century. The legions have retreated, leaving the inhabitants of the former empire prey to warlords. A Gothic overlord, Theodoric the Great, has restored some semblance of order in Italy, but his position is undermined because, as an Arian, he is a heretic in the eyes of the Roman and Orthodox Churches. He is, however, a tolerant monarch whose stature as leader is unquestioned.

The main character is a Roman Briton who has left his fine villa in southern England a smouldering ruin after a raid. He travels to Italy in search of law and order. He is befriended by Theoderic and also by Boethius, the greatest Roman of his day and one much honoured until the king destroys him.

Caught between two loyalties, the Briton is in peril but he has well-placed friends, both in Italy and in the eastern capital Constantinople.

Other notable historical figures woven into the story include St Benedict of Nursia, founder of the Benedictine Order, Clovis, King of the Franks, and Justinian, the great Byzantine emperor.

Set in the extraordinary time when great men were striving to restore some semblance of order after the collapse of the Roman Empire, *The Last Romans* unfolds a powerful and moving story. Its message is inspiring.

432pp **ISBN 978-1-84193-021-3** **£12.95 hb**

RICARDO'S LAW

Fred Harrison

'This is the fundamental reason … why the welfare state of the past 60 years has not worked' **The Guardian**

The Welfare State is the pact between people and their governments to abolish the evils of poverty and ignorance. 'Progressive taxes' are supposed to equalise people's life-chances, but Harrison reveals how wealth is transferred from people on the lowest incomes to asset-rich investors. Clues to the truth emerge as the author traces the effect of taxes used to pay for public services.

The process has remained unrecognised because the transfer operates unseen through the 'invisible hand' of market forces. Harrison exposes how this works by analysing the property market. Owners of high-value homes recoup what they pay in taxes quite legitimately through rising property prices.

Thus they effectively enjoy tax-free use of schools, hospitals and other amenities, while lower-income earners, and families that rent their homes, have to carry the cost of such public services without rebate. This is the reason why the rich grow richer while the poor grow relatively poorer.

Using Tony Blair's decade in power as the illustration, the author explains that this is a failure of governance rather than market failure – politicians have ignored the Law of Rent, also known as Ricardo's Law after the economist who provided the first scientific explanation of how it works.

320pp **ISBN 978-0-85683-241-3** **£18.95 hb**